HARD-DYING MAN

Caleb Frome and Drew Hatton's friendship had ended acrimoniously. Now fifteen years on, owlhoot Drew found bounty hunter Caleb on his back trail, for Drew had robbed the Santa Fe railroad train, killing an old Mexican peon. But because of their past closeness, Drew couldn't bring himself to kill Caleb, and suspected it was the same for his ex-buddy. Now in the desert, his horse dead and few bullets left, Drew must shoot Caleb Frome to save himself from the gallows . . .

ELLIOT LONG

HARD-DYING MAN

Complete and Unabridged

LINFORD
Leicester

First published in Great Britain in 2002 by
Robert Hale Limited
London

First Linford Edition
published 2003
by arrangement with
Robert Hale Limited
London

British Library CIP Data

Long, Elliot
    Hard-dying man.—Large print ed.—
    Linford western library
    1. Western stories
    2. Large type books
    I. Title
    823.9'14 [F]

    ISBN 0–7089–4975–4

Published by
F. A. Thorpe (Publishing)
Anstey, Leicestershire

Set by Words & Graphics Ltd.
Anstey, Leicestershire
Printed and bound in Great Britain by
T. J. International Ltd., Padstow, Cornwall

This book is printed on acid-free paper

1

Once more Drew Hatton single-fingered beads of sweat off his narrow brow. From this high point of the bluff he could see Caleb Frome was continuing to edge his way towards him through the cacti and mesquite down there.

There was a time when he and Caleb knew the deep bonds of friendship, forged of the steel and trauma of war.

Licking his cracked lips, Hatton squeezed his right hand tighter around the hot metal of his Winchester .44. Though the day was early, the sun was already a brassy fireball, threatening to draw out every last drop of moisture remaining in his lean, muscular frame. What moisture remained, that is, after Caleb Frome's implacable six-day chase after him across the dry ochre hills and semi-desert out there.

Hatton stared with bleak eyes at the

approaching figure and muttered foul obscenities. After barely escaping with his life from the Santa Fe posse's ambush, events after that still added up to nothing short of a catalogue of disaster. Hatton listed them in his mind. Three days ago he lost his horse, due to a broken fore cannon; two days ago he ran out of food; this morning he drank the last of his alkali-bitter water. Now he was down to two shells in his rifle. However, there was one consolation: he still had his fully loaded Colt .45 single-action, safely rammed into the plain, practical holster nestled against his right thigh. But, after that, he knew what further defence he could put up would be down to his Bowie knife, his hidden stingy gun and his bare hands.

And that brought home another bitter truth: he was near to total exhaustion after six days with little sleep, riding and walking over rough ground under a merciless sun, and Caleb just grinding relentlessly on behind him. It was only through accurate rifle fire — placing slugs of lead close enough to Caleb to make him think twice about coming on — that kept his former friend at a safe distance, like a timber wolf following its prey, waiting for it to die.

The first hint that Caleb was tracking him came soon after his escape from the Santa Fe posse's ambush in that unfriendly blue line of hills he could still faintly see, west of these dry, harsh lands. The running gunfight that followed the bushwhack turned out to be a short, brutal affair. And, as far as he knew, he was the only one to get out of the ambush with his life. But, if some of the other gang members managed it — the thought cheered him momentarily — well, he was ninety per cent sure they would be making their presence known pretty soon and would try to get him out of this damned hole he found himself in.

Even so, the fact that the Santa Fe posse *did* pull off the ambush and was now probably headed back to Santa Fe full of horse dung — saying they'd killed all of Drew Hatton's hardcase bunch — didn't answer the question of how Caleb Frome came to be on his back trail. Last he heard, Caleb was in Utah, hunting down the Jimmy Macher gang. Hatton grinned. Maybe Caleb wanted to prove the posse liars by taking in Drew Hatton himself, to claim the $5,000 reward put on his head by the territory authorities and the Santa Fe Railway.

Stilling his thoughts, Hatton reared up a little off the hot caprock of the bluff. Something altered the pattern of things down there. It was Caleb, easing his big, seemingly tireless black gelding down to a stop. At a guess, Hatton reckoned less than a quarter of a mile of desert lay between them now. And at this early hour, the air was still clear enough to allow him to watch as Caleb pulled a field telescope from one of his saddle-bags and put it to his right eye. With leisurely movements, Caleb began to study the broken rim of the bluff he was on.

Instinctively, Hatton pressed harder against the gritty rock. He sucked hard on the pebble in his mouth and swallowed the meagre saliva it created while he watched Caleb make a slow, meticulous sweep with the glass across the ragged rock line he was hidden on. From past experience of Caleb's trailing abilities, it was a sure bet his former partner already knew he was on this bluff, waiting for him, because, plain fact was, there was no longer any place else for Drew Hatton to go.

And fining it down, Hatton figured 400 yards now separated them. It was so tempting to get the killing of Caleb Frome done. With his new .44, and the sights set up right, he could take Caleb out, like he was a clay pipe on a shooting gallery. But, there was the dilemma: *Caleb Frome was the one man in the whole of this world he couldn't kill.*

He watched Caleb put his telescope

away, as usual, meticulously. What Hatton wasn't ready for was Caleb now taking a long drink from his canteen and making a big show of it. The damned man was even soaking his kerchief and swabbing his face and neck with it. And after that callous manoeuvre Caleb was now filling his hat and giving his horse a long, cool drink while letting large sparkling drops splatter on to the desert floor.

Sucking his pebble furiously, Hatton gripped his Winchester and glared down, his look glaze-hard. *The no-good sonofabitch!* What was he trying to prove? Goddamn, Caleb Frome was the last person on this earth he would expect to see pull a lousy trick like that on a thirsty man — a former friend at that! Damn it, there was a time he and Caleb rode the same trail; served together through the Civil War, under the Rebel flag — even rode the owl hoot together for a spell.

He was a fourteen-year-old, starving orphan with nothing to lose. He joined up with the first army he met. Major Caleb Frome was a mature Southern gentleman, with a cause to fight, commanding a company of men recruited from his own estates and equipped by him out of his own pocket.

For some screwy reason, Caleb took him on as a kind of juvenile *aide-de-camp* until he discovered that Drew Hatton, despite his tender age, could use a rifle or a sixgun with equal skill and could fight like a mountain cat, despite his puny stature. And after four years of bloody war, it turned out that the raggy-ass who wandered into Major Frome's camp at the beginning of the war was destined to finish up a lieutenant in his own right, after showing abilities to lead and inspire men to do his bidding at Chickamauga, as well as having a natural penchant for unconventional strategy — enough to impress General James Longstreet, to whose force Caleb's company was then attached.

But it was after the war that Caleb

sprung his biggest surprise. He saw no reason, he said, why they should split up just because the conflict was over.

'I'm going to adopt you, boy,' he went on, with a tilt of his stern chin, 'take you back to my estates in Georgia, introduce you to my wife and daughter, make you into a Southern gentleman. And, in due course, I'm going to get you married into a good family so you can raise kids and, in the fullness of time, take over the estates.'

Hatton was almost struck dumb. 'Me?'

Caleb grinned. An unusual event. 'Yes, boy. You.'

'What about your own son? Don't he count?'

Caleb arched his dark brows. 'You know very well what a traitor he became, joining the Union. When he did that, he was no longer my son. His death at Gettysburg was the best thing that could have happened to him.'

'You never told me he died at Gettysburg.'

This time Caleb's face was grave. 'No,' he said. 'Apparently, he died bravely. I have that consolation and it comforts me at times.'

Hatton stared down at the menacing figure on the desert floor below him. It was the way Caleb dismissed his own flesh and blood from his mind; as though he was throwing away an unwanted package. How could a man just blank out something as big as that from his mind because that person didn't go the way Caleb Frome thought he should? But when he got over the shock of the declaration to make him his son, he asked Caleb if he figured it was wise to go back to claim his estates, after Sherman's bloody, rapacious march to the sea. Rumour was, little was left standing in that once-fair state of Georgia, and surely nothing would be left for defeated Johnny Rebs to go home to.

The anger Caleb displayed was disturbing.

'It is my home, boy. My wife and

daughter are there. I have to go back.'

So they rode south. It came as a surprise to both of them to find the grand Frome mansion was still standing — white-pillared, proud and intact, after all the devastation they'd ridden through to get there. The downside though, was that it was occupied by an arrogant Yankee carpetbagger and his very large family. How Caleb held himself back from killing the sonofabitch right there and then still held some mystery for Hatton. But Caleb just made the excuse of asking the way to the next town and turned about.

But as they rode out of the gates Caleb said, 'Where is my family, boy?'

'You could have asked.'

'And tip my hand?' Caleb snorted. 'Damn it, boy, Federal troops are everywhere, as you know, and Johnny Rebs are fair game for a lot of these scoundrels. Got to be careful, got to talk to people I know and trust.'

After a deal of searching, and having to witness pure misery wherever they

10

rode, Caleb found a former neighbour he could talk to. He was in a similar position to himself — dispossessed by avaricious carpetbaggers who were backed up by a company of Yankee infantry garrisoned in the nearby town. It was headed by a Major Freebody who was as hungry as the carpetbaggers for a share of the spoils of war. And that wasn't the worst of it.

'About your family, Caleb . . . ' his one-time neighbour said. He paused. He seemed reluctant to continue.

'Just tell it plain, John,' prompted Caleb.

The neighbour shuffled. 'Well, Sherman's men stripped your place of everything. Just stark, plain looting it was. And I can only guess your folks thought they'd let you down badly when they lost your estates to those no-good Yankee carpetbaggers. Must have been the final straw for them. And, not having heard from you for nearly twelve months they . . . ' The neighbour paused, squinted at Caleb, clearly unsure about going on.

'Just tell it all, John,' encouraged Caleb, but his features were bleak, harsh.

The neighbour gestured with a hand. 'They went missing. When we found them . . . well, everybody came to the conclusion they figured you were dead and they no longer had anything more to live for. They — they hung themselves, Caleb.'

Caleb straightened his back. Hatton saw his friend's whole body quiver for a moment, before he said, 'Makes sense, John. Makes perfect sense.'

He swung up on to his horse. But Hatton went cold when he saw the terrible look that came to Caleb's grey stare at that moment of awful truth. Without further words, his former commander swung his big roan mare around and thundered along the byways that led back to his mansion. Hatton found he needed to use the quirt hard on his dun to keep up with Caleb's furious dash.

Reaching the grand house, Caleb swung his mount through the white gates, rode up the long drive under the canopy of moss-hung oaks and called for the carpetbagger to come out. When the arrogant bastard did and stood wide-legged between the tall white pillars, staring at the ragged Rebs with slight puzzlement on his round red face, Caleb shot him plumb between the eyes — right in front of the sonofabitch's wife and children, standing in the doorway behind him.

Their flight, with a company of Yankee cavalry on their tail, a $1,000 reward on their heads posted throughout Georgia, and the realization that they would have to take to the owl-hoot trail if they were to stay alive and eat regular, didn't, however, come easy to Caleb Frome.

As was his wont, Hatton grinned at the recollection. Fine for him, of course, since, from the age of eight, he had been required by circumstance to thieve, scheme and live on his wits after the Comanches killed his sister, ma and pa while defending their Texas small-holding. Why had he lived . . . ? Luck decided he should be out on the prairie, looking for quail eggs, when the Comanches ghosted in and did their deadly work.

But Caleb Frome, outlaw? No. Caleb Frome was brought up an honourable man, a pillar of Southern society. And until they parted a year later, Caleb continued to consider the owl-hoot trail totally unsuited to him and just a stop-gap measure until things got better and they could get back to living a decent way of life. Only trouble with that was: Drew Hatton didn't understand the meaning of a 'decent way of life', having never lived one.

Hatton lifted his dark brows. Give old Caleb his due, he did try hard to teach him how to read and write, be 'decent', be the gentleman, and he would always be grateful to him for that. It came in useful on occasion. And, because Caleb still considered him to be his son and all that entailed, despite everything, he seemed to figure that that also gave him the right to run his life, being only nineteen at the time.

Hatton shook his head and gazed a little sadly at the approaching figure. Why, even now, after being fifteen years apart, he fancied he could hear his ex-friend's stern disapproval of his latest venture — the plundering of the Santa Fe Railroad train at Saledos Junction and relieving it of the $25,000 payroll it was carrying.

'Have you finally gone totally to the devil, boy?' His eyes would be like gimlets. 'And did you have to kill that old *peón*, sitting out his *siesta* under the water tank, minding his own business, hurting nobody?'

'He was staring at me!'

'That doesn't mean to say you had to kill him!'

'He could identify me, damn it.'

'Boy, don't you realize? Your likeness is on every poster throughout the territory and beyond.'

'Those pictures ain't a bit like me!'

'Are not, boy — are not.'

Sonofabitch!

Abruptly fading the imagined scene at that, Hatton stared down at the man on the desert floor. How many times these past six days did he need tell to himself his friendship with Caleb Frome was long dead? That their partnership finished fifteen years ago when that goddamned bank job they were on went all to hell.

It was to be a routine heist, done half a dozen times to the usual formula: pick a hick town, wait for a quiet time, step in, draw guns, demand money and get out fast before the town knew what hit them.

Everything was going fine until the woman teller started screaming, 'Thieves! They're robbing the bank!'

She was hoisting up a cap-and-ball Remington she had pulled out from under the counter, and, holding it in two hands, was pointing it straight at him. Hatton fluttered his eyelids. *He didn't have any option but to kill the crazy bitch!*

They evaded the posse easily enough. Four days later, deep in the Arkansas backwoods by the camp-fire after supper, Caleb at last broke his long silence. 'You didn't have to kill that woman, boy.'

Shit, he must have been brooding on it all that time. Four goddamn days!

'The hell I didn't,' Hatton growled, his stare ferocious. He poked out a bony finger. 'Ain't you forgetting something, Caleb? She was about to kill me.'

Caleb's hand-wave was dismissive. 'We could have disarmed her easily enough. Didn't you stop to think for a moment, before you pulled that trigger, she could be somebody's wife, somebody's mother?'

Hardly comprehending, Hatton snarled, 'You being serious? What the hell's that to me?'

Caleb's stare was brittle. 'Is that all that taking life means to you, boy? Just

17

another corpse. Haven't I taught you anything?'

Hatton glared at that. 'You ain't making any goddamned sense, Caleb.' He had long ago dropped the 'sir' of army days.

Caleb's stare remained steady. 'You know I live by certain standards.'

Hatton snorted, 'Well, too damned bad for you is all I can say.' He glared sulkily across the flickering fire.

Caleb's pale gaze remained implacable, still trained on him across the flames. After moments he said, firmly, 'I want you to stop this mindless killing, boy. The war's over.'

Hatton curled his lip into a sneer. 'Well, is that right, old buddy?' He leaned forward, to show his growing contempt for Caleb's censuring. 'Well, d'you want to know something? I'm getting sick of you. And if you are going to keep on about that damned woman I'm going to quit on you, right now.'

Caleb was slow to take his short briar pipe out of his mouth and his tone was measured when he replied. 'Now, I can't allow you to do that, boy. You're still only nineteen years of age. I still feel responsible for you, figure you to be my son — '

Hatton interrupted, petulantly, 'Your goddamned idea, not mine.'

Caleb raised his thick brows. 'True. But, think on it, boy. We've been through a lot of things together, you and I.' He paused a moment, as if still pondering. 'You know, son, I figure there's a deal of good in you if you'll just give it a chance to come out. Thing is, I can't stand aside, to see you go off on some wild rampage, for that's what you'll do if I don't continue to take you in hand. Killing like that — without feeling — belongs to war. And you seem to have a natural ability to thieve. It's not good. Time you thought about that, come to terms with it and rejected it.'

Hatton round-eyed his disbelief, eyebrows arched. 'Is that so? Well, just what in the hell have you been doing recently, Caleb, if it ain't thieving? Tell me that.' He added, 'Mister, you're in this just as deep as me and it's time you recognized that. And it was you who shot that carpetbagger and got us into this mess, not me.'

Caleb nodded sombrely. 'Well, I can't argue with you there, but there was a strong, justifiable cause to that.' He paused and leaned forward earnestly, his usually grey, intense eyes lighting up with sudden enthusiasm. 'Boy, I want you to come along with me. Tomorrow we could start out for the West. Big country. Loads of opportunity. We could carve out a new life for ourselves, for, as God's my judge, if we stay here, we'll be obliged to live in outlawry for the rest of our short lives and I would not be able to come to terms with that. And I'm not proud of the fact I led you into it, either.'

Hatton laughed. 'Led me into it? Shit, I knew nothing else until I joined your rag-tag army, and look where *that* got me.' He folded his arms and stared moodily across the fire as it snapped and crackled between them, flickering light on to the pines standing around them in the dark night. 'I tell you, Caleb,' he went on after moments, 'I've been a natural-born owl-hoot since I was eight. Never knew that, did you? As for going West? Forget it. I got other plans in mind.'

'That so?' Caleb's expression changed perceptibly. 'Go on, boy,' he said. 'Don't stop there.'

Hatton tilted his chin arrogantly. 'Been thinking on it for some time,' he said. 'I've finally got to figuring you're holding me back. You just keep arguing me down all the time, keep making me feel like I'm good for nothing — that I ain't got an idea in my head. Well, come tomorrow, I aim to move up into Missouri, find and join up with Jed Kelly's gang. Jed won't be goddamn picking at me all the time, carping on about going straight. I hear he's been raiding into Kansas, making some real big hauls. That's got to be for me.'

Caleb's grey stare was doubtful. 'That murdering no account? You seriously mean to take up with him?' He stabbed out with the stem of his pipe. 'Boy, listen to me and think hard on what I'm about to say. We should move West, right now. We've got a nest egg. When we're settled in some nice little town and have a good business going, I'd like to see you get married to a nice, gentle lady, maybe have a few children. That's got to beat the owl-hoot trail by a mile.'

Hatton scowled. 'You reckon? And there you go again. Planning my life. Don't you ever let up? How about *you* getting some *gentle* lady and *you* having a mess of kids, uh — when I'm long gone, that is.'

Caleb's gaze remained level, calm. 'You know, lately I have never been much for the female gender, boy. I find it difficult to replace the memory of my wife, not that I want to.' He paused, raised his brows, shrugged. 'But, if the right one came along one day . . . well

. . . I'm not entirely averse to the idea of remarrying.'

'Is that so?' Hatton sneered. 'Well, Caleb, you're going to be doing it alone. Like I said, come tomorrow, I'll be heading for Missouri. If you ain't up for it, then here's where we part.'

Caleb stared for long moments. 'Don't do it, son,' he said quietly. 'Kelly is bad news. Think hard. Is that what you really want?'

Hatton glared moodily. 'Bet your damned boots it is.'

Caleb frowned down at the pipe in his big hand. It was a long time before he said, 'I find that a real pity, son.' With that he knocked the dottle out of his pipe and rolled into his blanket. Soon, he was fast asleep and all Hatton could do was stare across the fire at his back.

★ ★ ★

Staring down from the bluff, a deep emptiness filled Hatton. *Sonofabitch*

23

never did try real hard to talk me out of it. If he had have done . . .

He raised sweat-mottled brows. They'd met again, two years on. A chance encounter in an outlaw town in the Nations when Kelly, himself and the rest of the boys were resting up after successful raids on two Kansas cow-town banks. He didn't ask Caleb what he was doing in that lawless stinkhole — he just offered to stake a clearly down-and-out former friend to a meal, maybe a little cash to tide him over. He didn't even ask Caleb how he got to be that way.

Caleb merely stared at him with those steely eyes of his.

'I don't want your tainted money, boy,' he said. He squinted, went hip-shot, sighed even. 'You know, I've been following your lawless career with some degree of disappointment, son. So I'll say it once more, there's still time to quit. We'll make out.'

Hatton beat his fist on to the hot caprock. Even now, that insult about tainted money when he wanted to be kind to Caleb caused him to hurt, real bad. However, it wasn't long after that Jed Kelly got himself killed in a gunfight and he got to be the leader of the boys. And it was after that that he really cut loose, showed the world what Drew Hatton was really about. But, even so, he tried to keep in touch with Caleb's movements. He got news his old partner had moved to Texas; heard he eventually became *segundo* to a Texas rancher, trailing steers to Abilene and Hays before serving a long stint as a Kansas trail-town lawman. Information filtered through that Caleb had proved to be an even-handed badge-man, fair with whoever he dealt with. And it was said Bat Masterson couldn't speak too highly of him. Soon after, he heard Caleb had got married to a Dodge City milliner and almost straight after bought a ranch in Colorado somewhere.

It was three years ago. Hatton swallowed hard. *Goddamn, he didn't know the C bar F spread was Caleb's.* They were in Colorado. There was a posse on their trail. They needed fresh horses. The C bar F corral, they saw from the ridge they paused on, was full of good saddlers. But when they swooped down, the three C bar F boys around the ranch made a fight of it, ran for the ranch house, forted up.

While some of the boys saddled fresh horses, Hatton and the others kept the battlers in the ranch house occupied. Then, God in heaven, the building began to blaze. Maybe an oil-lamp got broken. Whatever it was, it was an accident. And for sure, he and the boys didn't know there was a woman and her kid in there. Only their terrible screams and their sudden appearance at the door, flaming like torches, told them that.

Hatton felt his gut knot up. There was nothing else he knew of to relieve their agonies but shoot them. It was those damned sonsofbitches cowhands, running for the ranch house and

26

shooting like that. They should take the blame for it, not him.

Hatton blinked sweat out of his eyes. What finding his wife and kid dead, and their having died in such a horrific way, did to Caleb Frome — and the fact he was not able to run down the perpetrators of it — only God knew. What Hatton did know for sure, though, was that it turned Caleb into this relentless manhunter he saw below him who had vowed one day he would find the men who did the killings. And when he did . . .

Hatton wiped a trembling hand across his dry, flaking mouth. He grinned nervously. So, in a way, it was ironical to have Caleb Frome trailing him for something entirely different — the Santa Fe Railroad haul — instead of that god-awful mistake in Colorado.

Faint gunfire suddenly crackled across the vast, dry country below, startling Hatton. He flicked his narrow gaze off Caleb and towards the racket. He saw trains of pale dust winding through the sparse vegetation down there and rising like twin banners above the semi-desert floor. One dust cloud suggested a single horseman riding hell for leather, the other many riders, similarly occupied.

Adjusting his gaze back to Caleb he saw his former partner was already swinging his big black horse around to stare at the oncoming riders. Hatton was not surprised to see Caleb gaze momentarily at the bluff he was on, as if in frustration, before heading for a low, boulder-strewn mound close by him — one of several dotting this arid country. When he was atop it, Caleb dismounted briskly and drew his big Winchester .45–90 from its saddle scabbard. Hatton narrowed his gaze. Goddamn, what he couldn't do with *that* gun, given the chance. But that wasn't the issue right now.

Swinging his gaze off Caleb, Hatton concentrated on the chase. He soon established that there were ten riders in the pursuing party, and it quickly became clear they were Indians. The one ahead of them was white and astride a clearly flagging horse. Every now and again the man would turn and fire off his handgun. Meantime, Hatton could see Caleb was now bellied down and in position on the boulder-strewn top of the lofty mound, ready to do some damage. And to confirm it, Caleb began shooting.

As Hatton expected, Caleb's firing was cool, methodical — like the man he always knew, Goddamn him! But, presented with the situation, Hatton already found his quick mind working rapidly. And the more he thought about it, the more his elation rose. This shindig could be the answer to all his problems. For there was a strong possibility those red bastards pounding across the desert right now could well be doing the job of killing Caleb Frome, relieving him of the trauma of that awful, future decision.

As was to be expected, Caleb soon settled into a rhythm of deliberate, selective firing. Clearly, his old partner wasn't going to make it easy for the redmen. Quick time, Hatton saw another redskin tumble out of his blanket saddle. Immediately, the chased rider turned his jaded mount and headed towards Caleb's position whilst continuing to cast desperate glances behind him.

Reaching the top of the mound, the hounded man dropped out of the saddle, drawing his rifle from its scabbard as he did. He bellied down beside Caleb. Faced with two steady guns, quick time, another redskin tumbled off his small, wiry mustang to lie still on the desert floor.

And it swiftly became obvious to Hatton that the redmen realized they were now in a vulnerable position. They swiftly backed off and dismounted. Two boys with the party — clearly having done it before — were gathering their ponies. They ran off with them into a dry arroyo close by. Dust clouded up as they went bounding down the steep side of the washout. In cover at the sandy bottom, the young Indians held the horses bunched while awaiting the outcome of the fight.

The fighting Indians immediately went to earth and began belly-crawling across the dry, rocky ground, making themselves as small a target as possible while they found defensive positions amongst the rocks, cacti and mesquite.

Savouring it, Hatton watched the manoeuvring. Soon the gunfire eased up considerably and the sniping began. He saw that Caleb and the stranger were now snaking away from each other, each clearly with the intention of finding better positions amid the rocks and to broaden their field of fire. And it soon became plain to Hatton that this could turn out to be a long, drawn-out duel. Indeed, the firing was now cooling down to sporadic rifle reports that clinked across the burning wasteland, as though specific targets were being sought.

After a short while, from his elevated position, Hatton watched another Indian rear, yell, drop down, begin crawling away, clearly hurt. Seeing it, Hatton narrowed his gaze. For sure, it was beginning to look as though there was a strong possibility that, despite the big odds they were up against, it could well be that Caleb and the stranger would come out the victors here.

And that wouldn't do at all.

Hatton turned his attention to where the Indian boys were holding the horses. If he could take them out he might well be able to get a couple of mustangs out of the manoeuvre — one to ride and one to rest — and get the hell out of here real fast.

Hatton blinked sweat out of his eyes, his expectations rising. The chances were good. Caleb's big black must be feeling the strain of the long hunt and wouldn't have much of a run in it, the other bastard he wasn't interested in. His mount was clearly near played out.

He rubbed a dirty hand across his dry, cracked lips. He reckoned 250 yards separated himself from the youths. He adjusted the elevation on his back sight and rested the rifle on to the hot rock he was lying behind. He had two cartridges in the Winchester. Man, a lot would depend on this and he would take his time over it. But one thing was in his favour — the boys were not suspicious of, or watchful for, the danger they were in. They were standing as still as the horses would allow them to, eagerly trying to catch glimpses of the situation between Caleb, the stranger, and their battling kinfolk.

Hatton allowed himself a wolfish grin. He was well known for his marksmanship in the army. This kill would be too easy. One inactive moment, and . . .

He sighted up the rifle, stilled himself, waited for the perfect chance. It soon came. He squeezed off. The first boy dropped with the abruptness of a head-shot mule deer. Hatton immediately swung the rifle on to the other boy. He was staring around, his face alarmed, apparently not knowing what to do for a moment. Again, Hatton squeezed off. The boy dropped like a pole-axed steer. As Hatton hoped, the released mustangs scattered his way — because of the vicious cacophony of gunfire going on between Caleb and the Indians scared them off going the other.

He scrambled up from his hideout, clattered down the shale of the eroding rear of the bluff. Soon he was crossing the desert floor and slithering down the arroyo's steep side to its sandy bottom. To his great joy one of the horses was already slowing down to a walk as it came trotting round the bend ahead.

Eagerly, Hatton positioned himself and waved arms. 'Ho! Ho! Easy, boy.'

The horse didn't seem keen on the idea. Fact was, Hatton knew he didn't smell Indian, he didn't look Indian, didn't sound Indian and it was odds on that all this nervous piebald mustang ever knew was Indian.

His quick anger flaring, he waved his

arms. 'Come here, goddamn you, hoss.'

The piebald white-eyed him nervously, evaded him easily and took off past him in a cloud of dust. Almost immediately, and frustrating Hatton further, three more horses came pounding down the washout and went thundering past, causing more dust to rise in a choking pall. Abruptly an Indian came running frantically out of the gritty fog. He was clearly trailing the horses.

Hatton reacted instinctively. With one fluid movement he brought up his Colt. The redman yelled harshly when he saw the situation he'd got himself into. He immediately began hoisting up his Springfield single-shot breech-loader, lifted from some dead Union boy, no doubt, Hatton thought abstractedly.

His first shot took the Indian in the gut, doubling him up. His next blew off the top of his head. Though fiercely proud of the emphatic kill, Hatton knew he didn't have the time to savour it. There were more important matters to deal with, for he knew he was fast running out of options.

He tightened his grip on his Colt and glared ferociously up at the rim of the arroyo, He fully expected to see his old mentor, or more Indians, come boiling over its ragged edge and pounding down the steep side towards him.

This wasn't going the way he'd planned at all, goddamn it!

2

To his relief, Hatton saw that the rim of the arroyo was clear.

He switched his gaze north, up the washout. He could still hear the reports of rifles — dull, whacking noises that dissipated quickly across the dry land. However, Hatton felt in his gut that the skirmish wouldn't last much longer. For sure, what was left of the redskin party would be getting anxious about their horses and wanting to be after them. Already, one brave had attempted it.

Hatton looked about him. He quickly realized his best chance was to get back to his own defence point on the bluff. Almost for certain, if Caleb did survive, the main business he was about — getting Drew Hatton — would be quickly resumed.

Another Indian abruptly rounded the bend in the arroyo. His bronze torso

37

gleamed in the sun and the muscles of his sinewy legs worked with smooth, effortless efficiency as he pounded through the dust, heading directly for him. Hatton also saw a Spencer carbine was clasped in his right hand. As soon as he saw him, the redman's face twisted into a mask of hate. He brought up his carbine.

Hatton composed himself, straightened his arm, sighted and fired his Colt with deliberate intent. And it was with satisfaction that he saw the Indian's savage grimace swiftly turn into a bloody, mangled waste as lead tore into his right cheek and exploded out of the back of his skull in an ugly spray of bone, brains and blood. The redskin's own lead went high.

Hardly had the whip-crack noise of the shots dissipated when Hatton saw another mustang come racing into view through the gritty haze that still swirled about in the stifling bottom of the gully. He couldn't believe his luck.

Hastily ramming his Colt back into

its holster, he managed to grab the strand of rawhide trailing from the horse's hackamore. He hung on, stomping his heels into the dust in a frantic effort to bring the beast under control. This time he was lucky and he eagerly swung up on to the rude blanket saddle on the pinto's back. With iron control, he began to fight down the beast's resentment.

Now, with grim urgency, he dug his boot heels into the horse's barrel, making it neigh harshly as it began to run down the arroyo. But the boom of a big rifle and the beast whistling its pain as it collapsed under him filled Hatton with new despair.

As he crashed on to the arroyo floor his head hit something hard, sending brilliant white light flashing across his vision, followed by pain and confusion. He fought to ward off unconciousness and gather his wits, while becoming aware of another rifle shot and what must be the last noises from the wounded pinto before its death. It could only be Caleb's doing, he decided. Desperately he clawed for his .45, hastily holstered moments ago, but a harsh command stopped him:

'Hold real still, boy!'

Hatton froze, his gut tingling. Face down in the gritty dust he became aware of the dry scrape of iron horseshoes on the sandy arroyo base. The noise stopped near his prone body. Hatton thought: *To pull my Colt right now would not be the most prudent thing to do and that's a fact.*

Awkwardly, he spread his hands. But, even in this inelegant position, and out of long habit when in danger, he grinned his unease.

'Kind of got me, ain't you, Caleb,' he said. He made it a statement.

The creak of saddle leather came, suggesting somebody dismounting. Moments later, Hatton felt something hard poking into his back. He had little doubt it was the business end of Caleb Frome's Winchester .45–90.

'Get up, boy,' Caleb said. 'And no tricks.'

Hatton rolled over. In spite of the fierce throbbing in his head, his muzziness and the glare of the sun in his eyes — which he tried to neutralize by lifting a hand to shade them — he managed to widen his smile. He looked up at the big-boned figure of his one-time mentor.

'Well, howdy do, Caleb?' he said with a breeziness he didn't feel. 'Seems you ain't lost your touch.'

He saw Caleb's severe face was, as usual, near expressionless. 'Can't say the same for you, boy,' he said. 'You continue to be a big disappointment.'

Hatton raised sweat-wet brows in mock innocence. 'How so, pardner?'

'You're still thinking with your ass, boy.' Caleb waved a hand vaguely up the arroyo. 'We were getting the worst of it back there until you shot the boys. Things changed mighty fast after that — when they got up to chase the horses and gave us something to shoot at.' A

41

hint of grim humour suggested itself in Caleb's flinty stare, before it faded and once more integrated with the hard, unforgiving planes of his face. 'Reckon I ought to thank you . . . but I won't.'

Disappointed anger flushed through Hatton, nevertheless he held his grin. 'Ain't it the way?' he said. He climbed to his feet and winced as waves of pain hammered across his head. His probing fingers found a lump the size of a quail egg near his left temple, as well as greasy blood. He felt like hell.

Caleb waved the rifle. 'Throw down your guns, boy.'

Hatton stared resentfully, but he found his jaunty confidence was quickly re-establishing itself now he realized he wasn't in imminent danger of violent death.

'That's asking a lot, Caleb, Indians about and all.'

His ex-partner glared his impatience. 'Get it done, boy. I'm not in the mood for debate.'

Hatton dropped his long gun, surprisingly still clasped in his left hand after his ungainly fall from the dead pinto. While he was doing it he said, 'I'd still like to know if you've finished off those hair-lifting bastards.'

Caleb's icy stare continued to express his intolerance to delay. 'It'll be done. Josh Crane knows what he's doing.'

Hatton raised his dark brows in mild interest. 'That other *hombre*? You know him?'

Caleb nodded briefly. 'I know him.'

Hatton chuckled harshly, cocked an eyebrow. 'I guess, in your book, getting your hands on a five thousand dollar reward is more important than helping a man finish off a bunch of Indians, uh?'

Frome's iron-hard stare fastened on him. 'You trying to rile me, boy?'

Hatton gaped to express innocent surprise before he said, 'Wouldn't think of it, pardner.' He screwed up his eyes and leaned forward and gestured with a grimy hand. 'This Josh Crane . . . he know about me?'

Caleb continued to glare. 'We didn't discuss you. We were too busy.'

'Guess so.' Hatton allowed himself another smile before he pursed his lips and said, 'So, now you got me, what you aim to do with me? Take me into Santa Fe?'

Caleb nodded sombrely. 'That's got to be the plan,' he said. He leaned forward, hard determination etched in his craggy features. 'Now, where did you cache the payroll, boy?'

Hatton narrowed his eyelids. It was out of long, sensible habit that the gang lay low for six months, hid the takings from any heist — except for a little living money — until things quietened down, but he didn't know it was known beyond the gang. However, Caleb always was a smart ass; able to figure things out.

Hatton cocked his head to one side, squinted. 'Think I'm going to tell you that, Caleb?' He chuckled. 'Well, you can sure go to hell on that one, pardner.'

Caleb continued to stare. Hatton found the gaze disturbing.

'Me go to hell, boy? Like I've explained to you in the past: it won't be me that'll be making that trip. You've already booked that ticket.'

Hatton grinned expansively. 'That so, pardner? Well, I heard most of the men you bring in these days end up over their hoss's saddles, dead as coyote meat. Wonder what the Lord'll make of that when you get to signing in up there?'

Caleb scowled. 'You shouldn't believe all you hear, boy,' he said.

But Hatton noted there was a tiredness about Caleb Frome. A world-weariness. A deadness. He smirked. 'The trouble is, I do!' He went hip-shot. 'So you're taking me to Santa Fe, uh? Well, that's a long ways to travel for one man guarding another and nobody to help him. Lot of things can happen in three hundred miles of lonely trailing, don't you think, old buddy?'

Caleb looked cynically amused. 'Oh, I reckon I'll manage, boy,' he said.

Hatton grinned. 'That so?' he said. 'Well, you'd better believe I'll be disputing that along the way, pardner. Real fierce. One thing is for sure — you ain't getting me to Santa Fe to hang.'

As though used to such pronouncements, Caleb pursed his lips, shrugged. 'Sad to say, but that's the end you've booked yourself in for, boy,' he said. He waved the rifle. 'Now, the sixgun. Shuck it.'

Still unwilling to leave himself naked in Indian country, but knowing there wasn't a hope in hell of Caleb agreeing, nevertheless Hatton desperately screwed up his face and blurted, 'I'll make a deal with you, pardner. I'll hand my gun over to you soon as I know those red bastards are dead or gone and it's safe to. That's fair, ain't it?'

Caleb looked vaguely amused. Slowly, he shook his head. 'You have no understanding of honour or fairness, boy,' he said evenly. 'That's a long-established fact. Now, for one last time: drop the Colt.'

Hatton made one last pleading gesture with his hands. 'But, Jesus, hell, Caleb, those red bas — '

An uncharacteristic growl of anger came from Caleb. He pointed the Winchester. He rasped, 'I'm going to start counting, boy. And three's the number to start praying at. *One . . .* '

Hatton howled desperately, 'Damn it, you've got to give me a chance to defend myself, Caleb.'

'*Two . . .* '

Frowning, Hatton flung the Colt .45 into the dust, alongside the Winchester already there and protested, 'Goddamn you, Caleb. You never did have any bend.'

Caleb waved the rifle again. 'The belt knife now, boy, and quick about it.'

Hatton glowered. 'Damn it, I need *something*, Caleb. Be reasonable.'

His former mentor hiked back the hammer. 'Do it!'

Scowling sulkily, Hatton tossed the long-bladed Bowie, honed to razor keenness, to the ground. 'There, goddamn you.'

Caleb waved the rifle once more. 'Now move away, boy.'

Glowering his wrath, Hatton complied. He watched as his ex-partner advanced, bent his knees and picked up the Colt and Bowie, while all the time keeping his gaze locked on to his own. Standing upright again Caleb thrust the Colt into his belt, the Bowie he placed into one of his saddle-bags, then he scooped up the rifle with his left hand. He stepped back, shaking the dust off it and stared at the dead Indian pony before returning his gaze.

He said, 'I take it you haven't got a horse.'

Sudden anger bit at Hatton. He glared. 'Shit. You being funny? You made damned sure of that, by God.' He scowled. 'A hell of a thing to do, Caleb — shoot a man's horse out from under him like that.' But again Hatton felt his oddly perverted need for occasional flippancy rise, despite Caleb's uncharacteristic cynicism. 'But, seeing as you've done it, maybe we should cut ourselves a steak or two for supper, uh?'

Caleb's gaze remained steady and unamused, though his lips did take on a sarcastic curl.

'You haven't changed much, have you, boy? But, your misplaced humour aside, that isn't such a bad idea. We've got a long way to go.'

Hatton shook his head in disgust as his jibe fell flat. 'Just no sense of humour, never did have. Goddamn it, man has to have a joke or two, else where would he be?'

Caleb squinted. 'Waiting on the gallows?'

Hatton glared. 'You don't let up, do you?' Of a sudden Hatton found he wanted to hurt Caleb, dig the knife in and twist it. And he knew he possessed the weapon to do it, though it might not be the most sensible thing to use at this time, but he was goddamned sick of his ex-partner already, high-and-mighty bastard.

'Heard you got your ranch razed to the ground, Caleb,' he said. 'The C bar

F spread, wasn't it? Sweet Meadows Valley, Colorado? Jees, too bad — your wife and kid getting burnt alive like that. Must have been the most god-awful thing for a man to come home to.'

He watched Caleb's iron stare go severely bleak.

'What do you know about that business, boy?' said Caleb.

Knowing his mistake right away and swallowing on his dry throat and sucking hard on the pebble in his mouth, Hatton said defensively, 'I heard talk.'

Without warning, Frome reversed his rifle. Hatton felt the brass-ended butt hammer into the pit of his stomach. Though jack-knifing to try and avoid the incoming wood and metal, Hatton felt pain explode through him. The blow was so savage it drove all the wind out of him and sent him sprawling to the arroyo floor. He lay gasping and retching, though there was nothing in his gut to bring up after near three days without food.

Fighting through his agony, he stared up. Caleb was towering over him. His face was a demonic mask, carved as if in rock.

'I asked you what you know, boy,' he hissed, 'and, by God, you'd better tell it.' Menace impregnated every word.

Hatton found he could do nothing but heave for some moments, but there was no let-up from Caleb. Hatton felt the rifle butt hit him again, in the ribs this time, dragging a harsh yell out of him. Despite his distress, his anger flared up.

'Damn it, Caleb, what's gotten into you? I just heard, is all.'

This time Frome raised his Winchester and aimed it. Behind the sights Hatton saw Caleb's eyes were grey, murderous slits, sunk into his gaunt head.

'I'm waiting for your reply, boy. It'd better be good.'

Hatton found his mind was now

51

desperately fumbling for answers. He knew in his gut if he didn't find the right ones he could be dead. Not in his wildest nightmares did he ever figure on meeting up with Caleb Frome and having to respond to a question such as this. And damn his own stupidity for reminding Caleb of his terrible loss.

'Why, it was in all the papers,' he blurted. 'You taught me to read the goddamn things, remember?'

His ex-partner's iron stare seemed to search every plane of his face, as if seeking out the faintest hint of insincerity. After moments he said, 'Yeah, I did. A fat lot of good came out of it.'

Hatton made a gesture of what he hoped came over as compassion, which it was. He didn't need to act on this one. 'I was sorry as hell about your loss, pardner. I truly was. You gotta believe me.'

But he saw his former partner's stare was void of any hint of friendship. 'Somehow, I don't believe you, boy, and that's a pity.'

Just then, without warning, another Indian came silently running around the bend in the arroyo. The redman stopped, his surprise clear, when he saw them and his black stare announced his snarling hate for anything white-skinned. And it was obvious that Caleb didn't know he was behind him. In that vital instant between surprise and savage action, the Indian paused. Hatton yelled his alarm, self-preservation as much as anything driving him. 'Behind you, Caleb!'

Frome turned with cougar swiftness. With deadly efficiency he drilled the redman dead centre of his forehead with a single shot from the Winchester — clamped against his hip. It was so sudden the Indian didn't even have time to get over his amazement. He gave out with a strange, heavy sigh and went down like a sack of potatoes, his rounded eyes staring into permanent oblivion. But in those few tense moments, Hatton realized he was presented with one of the chances he was going to have to look for if he was to avoid the rope in Santa Fe. He lunged for his Colt, stuck in Caleb's belt.

With a growl, his ex-partner leapt back, still agile as a wild cat and just as deadly. This time, Hatton felt the butt of Caleb's Winchester hammer into his chest, sending him sprawling into the dust, gasping for breath. At that moment another rider came galloping round the bend of the arroyo.

His gut jumping up into his mouth Hatton shouted, 'Caleb! Another one.'

However, in the same instant he recognized the rider as the man who, earlier, was being chased by the Indians. Even so, on his warning, Caleb swung around in a crouch, but almost immediately straightened and lowered his rifle.

'Josh,' he said.

Hatton found, close up, that Josh Crane was a man well in advance of middle age. His round, rugged face was weather-tanned to the texture of mature leather, a big part of which was covered by a grizzled beard. His lively blue eyes stared at him from under bushy grey brows. Josh's worn, baggy clothing suggested that his situation at the moment was not as good as it could be. In fact, Crane's attire comprised a battered slouch-hat, dark, grubby hickory shirt and pants, and a greasy brown jacket, the buttons of which were substituted by the tips of antlers, drilled and fastened to the cloth by thongs of rawhide and fashioned to slip through the buttonholes. However, despite this look of poverty, Hatton observed that Crane seemed able to afford plenty of bullets, judging by the half-full bandoleer across his chest.

Crane abruptly pulled his horse to a stop, stirring up a miasma of dust. He glanced at the dead Indian, then leaned forward and rested his hands on the saddle horn.

'Guess you beat me to it, Caleb,' he said. 'I was just about getting close enough to salivate that red varmint.

Last of them, far as I can judge.'

'Figured he might be,' Caleb said.

Hatton met Josh Crane's brief, mildly interested, glance as it once more turned on to him. And it was immediately clear that the oldster sensed something had been going on between himself and Caleb with him having to get to his feet and dust himself down.

Caleb was continuing, 'You're not about to complain about me knocking over that red son of Satan, are you, Josh?'

Crane swivelled his gaze back to Caleb. 'Hell, no,' he said, before he brought his look back to Hatton, who met it squarely. After moments the oldtimer screwed up his face and said, 'Seem to know your face from some place, mister.'

Hatton nodded. 'That's likely.' He grinned and added, 'I do have a habit of getting around.'

The old cuss waited a moment or two, then, as if disappointed he didn't get a name, he said, 'Well, it'll come, I guess.' He spat brown chaw juice. 'Me, I ain't so reluctant about my name. I'm Josh Crane. Been looking for colour.' He waved a hand at the snowy peaks north-west, rising out of the foothills bubbling up from the semi-desert. He crackled a laugh, phlegm gurgling somewhere deep in his chest, before he raised brows. 'I figure I was born to a hankering for gold,' he said. 'In the blood, I guess. Ma died when I was still knee-high to nothing. Well, when she did pass away, seems she was the only thing been holding Pa back, for, right after the funeral, he sold the farm, bought himself an outfit and trailed out, me sitting on the pack-mule, holding on for grim life. Over the years he took me to every damned strike found by man. Yes, sir. Montany Territory clear to Mexico and back again. You name it and I've been there.'

Crane paused, shook his head, his look turning a little sad. 'Sorry to say a grizzly done for Pa in the Sapphire

Mountains. The mean bastard tore Pa's head clean off — just afore he died from the effects of the three bullets Pa put into *him*.' Josh sighed regretfully. 'Took me some time to get over that I can tell you, being only fifteen at the time.'

Feeling a tad sorry for Josh's sad loss, nevertheless Hatton smiled inwardly. It seemed to him that Crane, like most lone-riding men when they got into company, just couldn't stop talking about everything and everybody, if allowed to. For sure, it might be a good idea to keep on the right side of this old-timer.

'Sounds as though your pa died brave,' he said.

Josh pushed out his chest proudly. 'Mister, Pa would have faced down Satan if it came to it.'

'That so?' Hatton ran his gaze over the prospector's ragged state. 'Appears you ain't been doing too well lately, Josh — poking around after that yellow stuff?'

Crane shrugged, pursed his purple lips and raised his grey-streaked brows. 'Temporary, just temporary.' He then nodded vigorously and added, 'I'll hit it big one day. You can bet your boots on that, young feller.'

Hatton grinned, despite his bruised head and aching body. 'Well, amen to that. I'm all for a man making his pile.'

Prospectors! Gold-crazy bastards, all of them. Always chasing El Dorado. Some would sell their souls for one good strike, or even to just get the hint of one.

Hatton stopped his cynical ruminations for a moment as a dazzling idea hit him with sudden force. *But, goddamn it, that driving yearning for golden riches could just be the card to get me out of this, played right.*

As his thoughts churned, Josh was waving a hand at the desert.

'My pack-mule's back there, somewheres. Let him go when them Apaches showed.' He nodded firmly. 'He'll be around again soon, you see if he ain't.

It'll take more than a goddamned In'jun to catch him when he's in that frame of mind, even though those red varmints is partial to mule-meat.' Here Josh paused, squinted from one man to the other. 'Say, do you two know each other by any chance?'

'In a manner of speaking,' Hatton said.

Caleb grunted before he said, 'Meet Drew Hatton, Josh.'

Instant enlightenment came to Crane's blue gaze. He gleefully beat his right fist into the palm of his left hand and grinned, revealing brown-stained teeth.

'Knowed it. Seen your likeness on the posters, though it ain't very good.' For moments, his appraisal was keen. 'Drew Hatton, uh? Well now, talk is you're a real hardcase. That so?'

Hatton shrugged, gave Crane his most disarming smile. 'Shouldn't pay attention to all you hear, Josh. Had things pinned on me I ain't been within a hundred miles of. Some say I'm a real likeable cuss — when you get to know me, that is.' He deliberately grinned at Caleb.

'You don't say?' Josh narrowed his gaze and leaned forward. 'So how come you've got five thousand dollars on your head, if you're so sweet?'

Surprising Hatton, Caleb cut in harshly, 'How come you know about that?'

Clearly startled by Caleb's tone, Josh lengthened his bearded face, leaned forward again and stared. Before he spoke he rested his gnarled hands on the horn of the old saddle over the roan's back.

'How?' he said. 'Called in Silver Wells for supplies the other week.' He cocked a thumb in Hatton's direction. 'They got Wanted notices all over the town regarding him and his latest escapade at Saledos Junction. That's how I know.'

Caleb's stare moderated slightly. 'I see.'

Crane squinted against the sun to meet Caleb's gaze and hitched in the saddle. He said, 'What you aiming on doing, Caleb? Take Hatton here into Santa Fe to claim the reward?'

Caleb nodded, admitted, 'That's got to be the plan.'

Josh scratched at his beard. 'Long way to ride and keep watch on a man, Caleb . . . alone, that is.' He waved at the peaks rising to the north. 'Those mountains are lonely places, and that's the way you'll have to go, if you're going to Santa Fe. Things have a habit of happening up in them sierras that ain't nice. We just killed off a passel of what you're likely to find up there just now. Bronco Apaches. Maybe you'll be needing some help getting Hatton through there.'

Caleb said firmly, 'I'll make it.'

Crane nodded vigorously, as if he didn't want to antagonize Caleb, but didn't want to let the subject go, either.

'Sure you will, but, thing is, I was figuring on riding up Santa Fe way myself, to try my luck in the San Juans. Been grubbing in these hills nigh on a year now. Not a trace of nothing. Just need a stake to get me going again.' Josh narrowed his lively gaze. 'How about twenty per cent of the reward, Caleb, if I ride with you? With the two of us to watch him, we could make the trip real pleasurable. And with that kind of money I'll be able to finance my next trip with some to spare. Got a feeling I'll be lucky this time around.'

Hatton listened keenly. For now, he would overlook being bartered for, like he was a piece of meat on a butcher's slab. Way things were shaping up, he could still get this situation working for him.

Caleb was gazing at Crane, as if deliberating with himself, before he said, grudgingly, 'I'll go to ten per cent.'

Crane screwed up his weather-battered face in disbelief. 'Only ten per cent? Goddamn, that's wild country up there, Caleb, but I know it like the back of my hand.' He poked out a finger. 'Still got snow up in the passes I'll have you know, besides Indians being about. And that's not to say there ain't other bounty hunters prowling around with the same idea you got. Five thousand dollars is a lot of *dinero*.' He gestured with his head towards Hatton. 'And, what about his gang? They'll be trailing you, if I ain't mistaken. Sure as hell, they ain't going to let this lie.'

'They're dead,' Caleb said flatly.

Crane narrowed his rheumy eyes. 'You stone-cold sure of that?'

'Sure as a man can be.'

Josh's grizzled face showed some relief but he said, 'Even so — *ten per cent*. That ain't much for a man to risk his hide for.'

'I ain't asking you to, Josh,' said Caleb. 'It was your idea.' He heaved a sigh. 'So, take it or leave it, old-timer. It's all you're going to get.'

Crane looked unhappy. 'Goddamn, you're a hard man to deal with, Caleb.' Again he waved at the mountains. 'Lot of risk up there, I tell you.'

Caleb said, impatiently, 'We got a deal, or not?'

Josh scowled. Hatton could see the

old-timer wasn't at all happy with the arrangement, nevertheless a resigned look came to the oldster's face and he said, grudgingly:

'Deal, I guess. I can just about make out with ten per cent, but it'll be damned hard.'

Hatton watched Caleb's face register his satisfaction.

'Then it's settled,' Caleb said. 'Now, see if you can round up one of the Indian horses for Hatton while I get things straightened out here.'

Crane stared for a moment, as if uncertain, then said, 'Well, you sure don't waste any time, once you got things your way, I got to say. I was planning on eating. Fighting off Injuns always makes me hungry.'

Caleb glanced briefly. 'We can eat tonight.'

Josh scowled, seemed about to say something in protest, but thought better of it. He wheeled his roan and headed out of the washout.

Hatton watched him go up the steep

side. Caleb agreeing to take Crane on board made things a mite awkward. Fact was, with only his ex-partner to escort him to Santa Fe, he was banking on a time when Caleb's concentration would slip and Drew Hatton would have his chance to take him and make a break for it. But, with two men sharing the responsibility, the odds on them getting the job done successfully were considerably improved, far as Caleb was concerned. Unless . . .

Hatton felt a warmth fill him. Prospectors liked gold. Had to, or they wouldn't spend their lives risking all kinds of hell scratching around God knew where looking for it. Like news of a lost seam being rediscovered, or information that a new El Dorado was out there and a map had been unearthed to point a clear way to it. Such news would send any self-respecting prospector loco. And to Josh it would be much better than the ten per cent Caleb was offering. Hatton grinned. Already, things were looking up.

Behind him, Caleb said, 'Kneel, boy.'

Hatton turned, his stare puzzled. 'Did you say kneel?'

Caleb's look was direct. 'That's what I said.'

Immediately, a ripple of nerves pattered across Hatton's stomach. He couldn't help but blurt it out, 'Why? You about to shoot me, Caleb, after all the preaching you done to me about *not* killing?'

Frome stared at him for some moments. 'You think I've sunk that low, boy?'

Hatton shrugged. 'You've got that reputation these days, I got to say.'

Caleb narrowed his gaze. 'I've already told you not to believe all you hear, boy.'

Hatton pursed his lips. 'Can't help it.' He stared at his old buddy. He saw nothing to fear in those calm grey eyes. He said, 'OK. If that's the way you want it. Got to say you got me puzzled, though.'

He sank to his knees. Caleb quickly

moved behind him. Hatton felt the warm metal of handcuffs being clamped about his wrists and immediately he protested.

'Goddamn, no need for bracelets, Caleb.'

He got no reply. Instead, he felt Caleb's hands now frisking his upper body and legs. Hatton cursed under his breath when Caleb's probing fingers found his twinbarrel stingy gun secreted in the pouch he had made for it at the top of his right boot.

Caleb said harshly, 'No need, uh?' Hatton heard him step back. 'Stand up.'

Hatton rose, turned and saw his old partner putting the Derringer in his pants pocket. Suddenly he felt mean, wanted to hurt again. He said, 'Going back to losing your wife and kid, Caleb — '

Frome's usually even voice sliced in, harsh and menacing, 'Bring that up once more, boy, and, so help me . . . ' Caleb let the words tail off. But he left no doubt about the threat of extreme violence if Hatton continued.

But Hatton attempted a look of innocence. 'I only want to express my sincere condolences, Caleb — '

Caleb had his Colt Frontier out, quick as light. Hatton felt it press hard against his right temple. 'Trying to rile me into making a mistake, boy?'

Nerves sparkling across his gut, snarling it up, Hatton said, 'Now, just how am I going to do that? Real intelligent man like you?' He waved his iron-secured arms. 'And me hog-tied.' He feigned a sigh, as if saddened by Caleb's reaction. 'Though we've gone our separate ways, old buddy, I still have good feelings for you. A man can't push the kind of thing we had going out of his mind, not ever. Leastways, I can't. Damn it, you were like a father to me those times, and we saved each other's lives more than a time or two in that damned war. So, when I read about your loss, I really did feel for your pain. I truly did.'

Caleb Frome's harsh laugh raked the arroyo sides. 'You think I fell off a plum tree, boy?' he said. 'You think I don't know what you're trying for? Drip, drip, drip. Eventually get me mad, drop my guard? You're a killer, boy. Nothing's ever going to change that. I'm not even going to give you an even break.'

Resentment welled up into Hatton's throat. 'Damn it,' he blurted, 'I could have killed you a dozen times back there, Caleb, but I didn't. I just wanted you to back off. Goddamn, you must have figured that out.'

Caleb admitted, 'Maybe I did, but it won't help you none, boy. You'll have to pay the price for your life of misdemeanours. The trail you've left behind you is too bloody to ignore.' But he took the Colt away, decocked it and holstered it. He went on, 'So, you see, there isn't much you'll be able to do, boy, to avoid the justice I'm taking you to meet. I'd advise you to just keep remembering that and make your peace with God along the way.'

Licking his incredibly dry lips and sucking on his pebble, Hatton felt the fence-wire-taut fear that filled him subside. After moments he said, 'You got any water, Caleb? Being up on that rock all that time waiting for you to come along — '

Caleb cut in, 'Yeah . . . up on the rock, waiting for me to come along. Did you have a mind to kill me, boy, seeing as you no longer had any place else to go?'

Hatton attempted a look of injured surprise. 'I swear to God, you got me all wrong there, old buddy. I was hoping you'd ride on by and that's the God's own truth.'

Frome said, his voice taut, 'And what if I didn't *ride by*, boy?'

Hatton feigned more injured pride. 'So help me, I'd have winged you, nothing more. Or better, just held you up and took your hoss.'

Caleb's cold laugh was almost sardonic. 'Got it all figured out, uh?'

Sudden anger spurred through Hatton. 'Always so sure, ain't you?' he flared. He took a moment to calm down. 'So, how about that water, Caleb? I'm burning up here.'

Caleb said, 'You'll wait, boy.'

Hatton's found his temper firing up once more. 'Damn it! My tongue's beginning to fill my mouth I'm so parched.' Caleb began fiddling with his saddle, as if to ignore him. Hatton snarled, 'Damn it, what's gotten into you? You lost your soul or something?'

Caleb paused in what he was doing and turned slowly. 'Maybe that's it, boy,' he said. He pressed a big hand to his chest. 'There is a hollowness, right here, like something's gone missing since my family was killed. Maybe it *is* my soul. It's a deep emptiness, filled with pure pain. It's a dead zone. I just can't fill it. And I know I never will until I find the ones who did that evil thing.'

A coldness filled Hatton. Knowledge that he and his gang were the cause of such agony in the one man he once respected above all others numbed him, as well as filled him with dread.

Caleb said, 'Lost your tongue for once, boy?'

Hatton almost jumped but he quickly regained his aplomb. 'Just don't want that damned Colt jabbing against my brain,' he said, 'if I say the wrong thing again.'

'Getting some sense into that head of yours at last, uh?' said Caleb. 'Well, good. Now, lie down, boy.'

Hatton stared. *'Lie down?* Why, damn it, I just got through kneeling!'

Without warning, Caleb slashed with the back of his bony hand. Hatton felt it cut, with stinging pain, across his left cheek. Reaching out now Caleb's big hand took a grip on the front of his dirty shirt. His ex-partner jerked him forward until their dust-coated noses were almost touching. Hatton could smell the rank tobacco on Caleb's breath. He knew his old commander liked a pipeful of an evening — kept his tobacco in a large, real fancy solid-silver box in his shirt-pocket. He could see the bulge now, back of his leather vest.

'You think you're being damned cute, don't you, boy?' Caleb breathed. 'Trying me all the time? Bringing up the fate of my family, et cetera. By God, deep down, you must hate me real bad.'

'*Hate you?*' Amazement filled Hatton. He shook his head fervently. 'So help me, you've got me all wrong there, Caleb. And my regret regarding the death of your family is genuine. Honest to God.'

He watched scorn fill Caleb's grim features before he said, 'You really expect me to believe that?' Hatton felt Caleb screw up the front of his shirt even more, enough to cause him to choke slightly as it tightened around his neck. 'But, since you keep bringing it up, boy, you've got me growing curious. So, I'm going to ask you once more: what do you know about the death of my wife and daughter?'

Once more Hatton felt worms of fear wriggle across his stomach. 'Nothing I tell you! Only saying what I read in the newspapers.'

Caleb's stone-hard stare bored into him, raking deep, as if to reach into his soul. As if it still found nothing, he seemed to relax a little. He said, 'All right, boy. Now, get down on the ground like I asked you to.'

Once more, anger flared up in Hatton. 'Goddamn, I don't see why the hell I should. Get up, lie down, kneel . . . '

Abruptly, Caleb released his grip on his shirt and moved behind him. Almost immediately Hatton felt the butt of Caleb's rifle crash into his back, again driving all the wind out of his lungs. Yelling out his pain he went face down and hit the floor of the arroyo. The agony he felt was exquisite as his right cheekbone cannoned into a small rock. Though still part-stunned he realized Caleb was fumbling with his legs. He felt the tug of ropes being tightened about his scuffed up saddle boots, pressing them so close together, ankle bone banged against ankle bone.

He howled, 'Goddamn it, take it easy, will you?'

Now trussed up and helpless, he lay cursing. The sun began to beat down on his back. The bottom of the arroyo — already hot — was beginning to take on the furnace heat of what hell's kitchen must be like, were he eventually to go there. He also realized his hat had come off and the sun's rays were now eating into the back of his head like probing red-hot needles, despite his thatch of long, black hair.

'I need my hat, Caleb,' he yelled into the grit of the arroyo bottom.

He heard Caleb moving. Moments later he felt his hat being jammed on his head. 'Be back shortly, boy,' his ex-partner said.

Panicking, Hatton heard Frome mounting his handsome black horse. Ignoring the pain it caused him he screamed out, 'You can't leave me like this, Caleb. I got to have water. And there's goddamned Indians about. No telling what they'll do. Could ride straight in on me. Hell, you know what they can do to a man when they catch him. You listening to me?'

The clatter of iron-shod hoofs receding was Caleb's only reply.

3

Hatton figured it could have been an hour — maybe even two — he lay in the bottom of the arroyo, the rays of the sun threshing down on him, eating through his clothing, digging claws of fire into his back and frying him up generally, before he heard movement again. It drove away the awful illusions he was beginning to experience in the fogging of his mind about Indians skinning him alive and slow-roasting him over a small fire.

He managed to struggle over on to his back. The effort left him drained and panting and trying to shield his eyes from the glaring sun by turning away from it. He saw it was Josh Crane riding towards him from the south, up the washout. He was towing behind him a pinto mustang and a pack mule. The mule had on its back all the trappings a prospector would tote along.

Almost sobbing with relief, Hatton croaked over his thick tongue, 'Got to have water. Josh. You got to allow a man water, not like that bastard out there.'

Josh got down off his roan, glanced at him and lifted his canteen off the saddle horn. 'Get you comfortable first, son,' he said.

Dragging him, he got him propped against a boulder, then he put his hand against the back of his head and eased it up. Hatton felt the water trickle on to his lips. He lapped at it eagerly, swallowing it down his arid throat. Too soon Josh eased off. 'Not good to take in a whole lot at once, boy,' he said. 'Sip it, real steady. Let it soak your mouth, then ease it down your gullet.'

'Don't tell me how to drink damned water!' Pain ripped at Hatton's throat. But he knew the old-timer's advice was good. After three more good sips, Josh bathed his burning face — causing him to moan his relief — then left him and started fiddling with his pack mule while talking to it affectionately. When he returned, he gave him more water until he said, 'That's enough. More in a while.'

Hatton sighed as Josh eased his head down. 'So help me, I won't forget your kindness, Josh,' he said.

He heard Crane's quiet, cynical chuckle. 'Yes, you will, boy,' he said with sureness, 'first chance you get to escape.'

Hatton shook his head weakly. 'Honest to God, Josh, I won't hurt you none if I do,' he assured.

Crane chuckled again, sceptically. 'Yeah, yeah. Sure. Heard some folks say pigs can fly, too.'

'Scoff if you like,' Hatton said. He stopped. It hurt to talk. His tongue was still slightly swollen, his throat raw.

Josh was saying, 'After sixty-three years of living, son, I've got a bit leery about taking such vows seriously.'

Hatton scowled earnestly. 'Josh, when I say something, I mean it.'

Crane nodded affably but was clearly unconvinced. 'Best thing you can do right now, son, is to try and rest your throat.'

He walked off to his pack-mule. Minutes later he came back and gave him more water. But during the time Hatton lay burning up on the arroyo bottom, he did not allow himself to be idle. He worked out a real cute plan and it was time to start trying it out. He grinned at Josh.

'Talking about a man being grateful, Josh,' he said, the water having relaxed his throat, 'met a fellow once, up in the Sangre de Cristos. Prospector, just like you. Dying he was. Well, I done him a favour, stayed with him until he gave up the ghost; made him comfortable, best I could. You know how it is. Man has to do what he can in situations like that. And it was while I did he told me of a location where he'd found gold. Whole seam of it, thick as your arm, so he said, right there in the rock, just waiting to be hacked out. Well, because of my kindness to him during his last hours, he said it was mine if I ever felt like going in there and getting it out. Drew me a map, everything.' Hatton managed to grin disarmingly and shrug. 'But, being in a different profession to him, so to speak, I kind of forgot about it.'

Josh stared down, disbelievingly. 'You *forgot* about it?'

Hatton could see that greed as well as rampant curiosity was already filling every line of Crane's seamed face. He nodded. 'Uh, huh.' He attempted another grin and sighed. 'I took his story with a pinch of salt. You know these crazy prospector tales — no offence to you, Josh, of course — going on about finding riches beyond their wildest dreams — '

'No, no, goddamn it,' interrupted Josh, waving a hand. 'He could have been serious. In fact, I'd bet on it. You done him a favour, see, boy — making his dying easy. It'd make a lonely man real grateful — that kind of thing. I know, being one. He'd be serious, all right. I'd wager my goddamned life on that fact.'

Hatton pretended interest for a moment. 'You would?'

Crane narrowed his eyelids and bent eagerly forward, his belief that such things could not be ignored clear. 'Didn't you even check on it?' he said, amazed.

Hatton shook his head. 'Naw. In fact, I thought no more about it. Just figured he was some crazy old galoot with a dream in his head that never came true. Kind of wishful thinking, you might say.'

Josh shook his head vigorously. 'No! We ain't like that, I tell you. Me being him, I'd have done just the same, like I said. You bet. I'd see that a man who done me a kindness like that'd reap the benefit of my labours, if I couldn't myself. There's a kind of pride in prospecting, you know, son. Sometimes, finding gold is just as important as getting it out. Kind of proves you were right all along and you ain't some sun-crazed bum. I tell you, it was his way of letting the world know he'd struck it real big, even though he'd never get to reap the rewards himself.'

Hatton held Josh's gaze for some moments before he shook his head once more. 'Naw. He was delirious, old timer. Fevered, most of the time. Just rambling.'

Josh shook his head even more vigorously. 'He was telling you the truth, goddamn it. You gotta believe me . . .'

Caleb rode in. He sidled the midnight-black up close and dismounted. As he did he said, 'Figure we should be riding on. I can't see no Indians. Guess what there was left have lit out for far places.'

Though he looked guilty for a moment, Crane soon adjusted his grizzled features. He gave Caleb a stare of hurt pride. 'I told you I got them all, didn't I?'

Caleb nodded, raised brows. 'You did.' Turning he bent and Hatton flinched as his old buddy reached for his shirt front and heaved him up to his feet. 'Bring over the Indian horse you got, Josh,' Caleb said.

Josh did as he was bid. Hatton had already observed that the beast was a handsome and frisky pinto mustang, Indian broke. Abruptly Caleb hoisted him up and draped him over the horse's blanket-covered back, face down. The beast played hell for a while, until it was soothed. Rope was then fastened to his hands and passed under the animal's barrel and knotted around his feet.

Anger warmed Hatton. *Trussed up like a damned chicken*! He rasped hoarsely, 'Jesus, you really have grown into a real mean cuss, ain't you, Caleb?'

From above him, Caleb's reply was even. 'You've got into a bad habit of using the Lord's name in vain, boy,' he admonished.

Hatton cursed.

When they rode out, Caleb led the Indian horse with one of the rawhide reins attached to a crudely plaited rawhide hackamore. Hatton found the pain he was already suffering, because of the use of the rifle butt about his body, was now enhanced threefold by his position on the horse. But he could only stare at the stony ground as it passed under him, his inhibitions about shooting Caleb sorely tried.

4

By dark they were into the mountains and camped in a clearing by a stream. Despite climbing steadily for the last hour before they stopped, Hatton reckoned they were still low enough, altitude-wise, to have aspens and cottonwoods growing around them.

He winced. His body was a hotbed of pain. Bruises ached across his chest and thighs, everywhere. The day's awful journey, draped over the back of that Goddamned Indian pinto, had proved to be pure agony — even so, his hunger was satisfied. Surprisingly, though he wouldn't take off the manacles, his old partner fed coffee, beans and bacon to him. The coffee burned at first but, after cooling, soothed his tongue and throat, enough for him to feel able to talk freely and without too much discomfort. Now, supper over and with his back leaned against a tree on the other side of the fire, Hatton observed Caleb was filling his pipe with tobacco from his silver case. Josh Crane, on the other hand, was lounging with his back against a tree bole, a mug of coffee couched in two hands, as if he was warming them. Hatton observed sourly that both men were seated comfortably, relaxed and enjoying the cool night air. Deep in the mountains that rose behind them, Hatton listened to the wolves chorusing their soulful songs, telling of far, lonely places and primordial savagery. Occasionally Hatton caught Crane gazing across at him, as if he was trying hard to figure him out. He decided he just couldn't let this peaceful scene continue.

'I'm hurting, Caleb,' he griped. 'Can't you take these cuffs off me so's I can wash myself down in the creek, massage myself a little — loosen up?'

Caleb glanced up, briefly from filling his pipe. 'Save your breath, boy.'

Hatton glared. 'Damn it, I need to

get some of this sweat and trail dirt off me. Even you can't deny a man that small comfort.'

The stream they camped alongside gurgled tantalizingly by. When they had made camp here at sunset an hour and a half ago, straight off Hatton decided the brook was just right for a man who liked to keep himself clean.

On hearing his plea, Josh stirred, spat, gazed at Caleb, a hint of disapproval in his look.

'Gosh-darn it, Caleb, if he wants to wash, let him. I'll stand over him with my rifle, if that's what's bothering you. No reason, as I can see, to give the man such a hard time — over a little thing like that, anyway.'

Though grateful for the intervention, Hatton still stared across the fire at Caleb, his look bitterly resentful.

'Josh's right, goddamn it,' he said. 'Good job somebody has some human feelings around here.'

Caleb studied him for long moments, then he got up and walked around the fire to him. He untied the feet first, then unlocked the wrist manacles. He turned and stared at the prospector.

'You got him, Josh. Make a hash of it and you can start packing, if you're still living, that is.'

At this apparent softening, a glimmer of hope stirred in Hatton. So, Caleb still had some bend in him . . .

The restrictions off him, the first time he tried to stand he collapsed into a heap, pins and needles rampaging through his blood-starved limbs. Eventually, he hobbled down to the waterside, gingerly peeled off his clothing and rinsed the grime off them. When he returned to the fire, he spread the clothes to dry. Standing by the blaze, Caleb was lighting his pipe with a glowing spar. Seemingly satisfied that the briar was well kindled he went back to his seat, trailing fragrant tobacco smoke back over his wide, powerful shoulders.

Back at the creek Hatton dropped into the pool formed by the water bouncing down the lofty crags at the back of them from the mountains' higher reaches. Entering the brook's icy coldness electrified him, caused him to gasp, but it was also intensely exhilarating. And wafting in from the dark meadows beyond the perimeter of the camp-fire he smelled the perfume of the mountain flowers and the knee-high sweet grass abounding out there in the dark night.

Enjoying the stimulation the water gave, Hatton massaged himself while Josh came to the waterside and seated himself on a mossy rock. He placed his rifle across his thighs to free his hands. Hatton watched now as Crane shaved a chaw off a plug of Brown Mule, popped it in his mouth and chewed a while before he spat. Wiping a stray streak of spittle off his chin, the prospector said:

'Never been too partial to water myself. Pa always said too much bathing tends to weaken a man.'

Hatton chuckled indulgently. 'Times I've heard that! Well, I wash every opportunity I get, old timer, and it ain't ever done me no harm.'

As if already sick of such mundane chatter, Caleb grunted, got up, stuck his stubby pipe between his strong teeth and, puffing more clouds, walked the hundred yards across the park to the rope picket-line, to which the hobbled horses and mule were tethered. Each animal chewed on grass cut earlier by Josh, using a sickle he'd earlier dug out of his bag of possibles.

Hatton latched his gaze on to Caleb, watched him begin currying the big black horse he called Black Velvet. Satisfied his ex-partner would be occupied for a spell he returned his stare to Josh Crane. The old-timer was also occupied with gazing after Caleb. When the prospector appeared to satisfy himself that the distance between themselves and Caleb was enough, he turned and said:

'The map to the gold we were talking on this afternoon, son . . . you still got it?'

Hatton felt cautious optimism well

up in him. Already it seemed Josh was swimming like a mesmerized trout towards a glowing bait.

'Not on me, I ain't,' he said. 'Put it in a bank in Tucson. They got strongboxes a man can leave his valuables in until he has a need to get them out again.'

Josh stared, clearly surprised. 'That a fact? Well, I got to say, you got a bald cheek doing a thing like that, being in the profession you are and all.'

Hatton laughed. 'You reckon? Well, hell, old-timer, I ain't about to rob myself, am I?'

Josh's stare rounded. 'Maybe not, but somebody else might think of doing it, and then they'll get the map. You thought of that?'

In pointing it out, Hatton reckoned Crane thought he was making a clever observation. He pursed his lips.

'Wouldn't matter a damn if they did,' he said. 'Like I said, I don't lend much credence to that map — or the story behind it. It's got to be a lot of hogwash

93

— the sad ramblings of a dying old man.'

Josh's stare turned immediately resentful. 'Mister, there you go again; disbelieving folk.' He rocked moodily on the boulder he was sitting on, while sucking on the wad of tobacco tucked in his left cheek. This time his gaze looked suspicious. He spat. 'You know, I'm getting a gut feeling you're making all this up, just so's you can trap me into freeing you. Am I right?'

Naïve ain't the word. Hatton gave him his most innocent, wide-eyed look.

'Holy molly, does it come over like that, Josh? I got to admit, that possibility hadn't crossed my mind, until you just mentioned it.' He rubbed his dark, unshaven chin. 'But, yeah, thinking on it from your point of view, I guess it could look that way. However, I can tell you right now — it ain't. I just reckoned I'd talk to you about it, find out what you thought, seeing as you're in the same kind of business, so to speak.' He leaned forward and cast a wary glance at Caleb before returning his gaze to the old sourdough. He said, confidentially, 'Truth be known, Josh, you're the first person I've ever mentioned it to.'

Josh screwed up his weather-beaten face. His look was still distrustful, nevertheless he said, 'So, you really *ain't* making it up?'

God almighty, this old bastard's been in the hills so long he wouldn't suspect a Rocky Mountain yarn if it kicked him in the teeth and drummed 'Dixie' on his rib bones. Hatton rounded his stare. 'You think I'd do that with old Caleb around? Lie to you just to get you to cut me free?' He nodded in Caleb's direction. 'Damn it, old pard he'd kill you right off, if you so much as tried a stunt like that. And I sure don't want that on my conscience. No, sir.' He sucked in a deep breath. 'No, it's like I said, Josh: I just didn't believe that old man's story. Just thought I'd sound you out about it, that's all.' He leaned forward, confidential again, almost whispered, 'The bald truth is, old-timer, I've gotten sick of the owlhoot trail. I'm wanting to get out of it, go straight. And, if there is gold where that old man said there is and we could get it out . . . ' He paused, sighed and allowed his face to go solemnly sincere, even a little sad.

'But, hell, what's the use of talking about it? My dreaming won't matter a damn now, I guess, for I sure don't expect you to go back on your agreement with Caleb — even if you could stand to get half of everything we dug out of that mine if you chucked in with me. Providing it's there, that is.'

Josh's eyes snapped wide open before narrowing greedily.

'Did you say half?'

'Uh, huh — if it's there, of course. Which I doubt.'

Josh rubbed his nose. 'That's a mighty handsome offer. Yes, sir.' He fidgeted uneasily with his rifle, spat more juice. 'And I'll tell you again, boy, that old-timer's story'll be right. I got no fears of that score. As for going back on my word . . . ' Crane spat again, rubbed his bulbous nose once more, looked at his badly worn boots. 'Well, it's not the kind of thing I would naturally do, not without a lot of heart-searching first. Truth is, I'd be mighty reluctant to do so, no matter what the incentive was.'

'Sure you would,' acknowledged Hatton. He insinuated more sincerity into his voice and features. 'And I wouldn't want you to, not on my account. Hell, a man's word's got to be his bond.' He leaned forward. 'But, after you've done your heart-searching, you about to say you might just consider it?'

Josh's look was startled when it came up from viewing his boots, as if he was suddenly realizing it really might be possible that he was being subtly manoeuvred into something he'd rather not be in. 'No, I ain't saying that,' he growled irately. 'But, on the other hand, I got to admit, Caleb ain't been over-generous with his percentages. Fact is, he's been downright miserly. Damn it, I'll be doing just as much watching as he is, maybe more so. Am I right?'

Hatton nodded vigorously. 'Right as a summer breeze, Josh. I reckon old Caleb's been real mean with the transaction.'

Crane scowled at him. He fidgeted some more. 'But, then again, Pa always said a man shouldn't cheat on a promise, once he's made it. And I got to admit, Pa was usually right about most things.'

Hatton said, as if surprised, 'That what he said? Even all that time ago? Well, damn it, we could have had the same pa, you and me, old-timer.'

Hatton began massaging his body as energetically as his painful bruises and stiffness would allow. The cold mountain water was beginning to bite in, numbing his hurts and making the rubbing more bearable.

After moments he said, 'Yeah, I guess

the old man's tale was just horse dung, anyway. Way he told it, you'd think he'd found the biggest strike since Sutter's Mill. He even said it was. But who's going to believe a cock-and-bull story like that, and from an old man half out of his mind?'

As if galvanized by this new information, Josh's blue, alert gaze reached across the fire-illuminated space. 'Did you say *Sutter's Mill*? The one that started off the 'Forty-nine Californy Gold Rush?'

Hatton nodded, pointed a long finger. 'That's the one. That's what he said. He added his find could even be twice as big as that. Seams as thick as your wrist, he said. But, like I explained before, my reckoning is, he was just bad fevered. A rambling, sick old man who never made the big one and was trying to make out he had.'

Josh shook his head vigorously. 'No, no, damn it! I know my own kind, if I know anybody at all.' With slightly trembling fingers, the old-timer scrubbed his grizzled chin. Hatton could almost see the battle between loyalty and greed fighting for supremacy in Crane's mind. Josh waggled an encouraging finger.

'And this Tucson bank — the one you got the map stashed in? You really *ain't* making that story up?'

Hatton made his expression appear hurt. 'Hand on heart, old-timer. And it just breaks my heart to know, now you've more or less confirmed it, that after a week or so's riding I could be in that town and have that map right here, in the palm of my hand — if I weren't in the fix I'm in, that is.' He made his look miserable and sighed to match it. 'No chance of that now, I guess.' He nodded towards the horse-picket-line. 'Old Caleb there — he's got all set to get me to Santa Fe and there ain't nothing going to stop him. And I don't expect you to go against your principles just for me, like I said.'

Clearly embarrassed, Josh moved uneasily on the rock he was sitting upon. Dropping his stare to his boots

once more, he said, 'Yeah, well, I . . . '
However, after moments, he snapped
his gaze up again. 'But, by God, I'd give
a lot to find out if your story really was
true. Ain't no harm in that.' He waggled
his finger again. 'This fellow you're
talking about . . . he give you a name? If
you got a name, I'd know for sure he
was straight. I must have bumped into
him some place or other over the years
— being in the same line of work as
him. And I've always been pretty good
at judging a man's character. I'd know
whether he was the kind of man you
could trust or not.'

Inwardly laughing at *that* claim, but
remaining solemn, Hatton shook his
head regretfully.

'Well, that's a shame, because we
never did get round to trading names. It
didn't seem important. Guess I was just
too busy making his passing as
comfortable as I could, while he was
trying to draw the map to pass on
where he'd found the gold.'

Josh shook his head, as if with

considerable regret. 'Damned pity.' He looked glum for a moment, before brightening up once more. 'What did he look like? If you can describe him, maybe I can put a name to him.'

Hatton pursed his lips, sucked in night air. 'Hard to tell.' He swilled water across his sun-seared neck, then waved a hand. 'He was a short cuss. Around five-four. But drawn, real ill-looking — which he was, of course. Job to tell how he'd have looked when he was well.'

Josh's face showed disappointment. 'Yeah, guess so. Five foot four, you say? That ain't much to go on.'

Hatton pursed his lips again. 'Reckon it ain't.' He sighed. 'Sorry, old-timer.' He ducked under the water and massaged his thick dark hair. When he came up again, Crane was casting furtive glances across the park towards Caleb, who was now plainly visible in the light from the risen half-moon and the fireglow. Following the old-timer's stare — and instantly annoying him

— he saw his ex-partner was already finishing off currying his big black horse.

'Looks like old Caleb's fixing to return,' he said. 'Pity we didn't get to talk a while longer, old-timer; reach some sort of agreement.'

'Yeah . . . ' Crane swung his stare off Caleb and on to him. He appeared nervous now, but he said urgently, 'About your offer — half the gold; what if I was to find some way to set you free, would you . . . ?'

Caleb's shout across across the park cut off the rest of what the sourdough was about to say. 'Get him out of the water, Josh. He's had long enough.'

Immediately, anger burnt through Hatton, but he hid it well. He fixed Crane with his black gaze. He said, suppressing the urgency he felt. 'You were about to say, old-timer?'

But Josh was getting to his feet, the look of greedy conspiracy wiped from his grizzled features by Caleb's harsh instruction.

'Nothing,' he said. He shouted back across the park, 'Right away, Caleb.' Hatton met the old-timer's stare when he turned anxiously to him once more. 'Better do as he says, son.'

Something amounting to desperation built up in Hatton. 'But you ain't finished what you was about to say — about freeing me.'

Crane shook his head, looked a little scared. 'Told you it was nothing. Got carried away for a while there, I guess.'

Hatton felt the urge to go for the old-timer, risk being shot, overpower him and make a life or death run for it. But that would be crazy. Fact was he now knew Josh Crane was malleable and, given time, could be persuaded. He forced a tolerant smile.

'Guess we both did, Josh. And, like I said, I never did believe that old man's story.' He scoffed, 'El Dorado, for God's sake!'

While flicking a glance at the approaching Caleb the old-timer hissed out of the side of his mouth, 'There you

104

go again. I reckon there's got to be some truth in it.' He dropped the level of his voice. Hatton saw his gaze was round and apprehensive as he watched Caleb advance across the park. But it was conspiratorial when he returned it to meet his own measured gaze. He breathed, 'If I do have a change of heart — which I ain't saying I will mind — Caleb don't get hurt in the break? Do I have your word on that?'

Hatton felt the warmth of triumph fill him. 'Swear it on a stack of bibles, if you like, Josh. Why, I'll have you know, I got a soft spot for old Caleb myself. I promise you, all he'll suffer is a little hurt pride when we tie him up just tight enough so's we can make our escape good. And what's that, I got to ask?'

Though he looked unhappy, Josh said, 'Nothing, I guess.'

Hatton narrowed his gaze. It wasn't a promise hard to make. For, the crazy thing was, he didn't want Caleb hurt — not by his hand anyway. But, if somebody else got the job done? Well, it

105

wouldn't be on his head, or mind for long. Feeling a thrill of anticipation running through him, he stepped out of the creek and went to the fire.

His limbs were now trembling, but they were also tingling and invigorated. He briskly rubbed himself down with some old, dry grass before pulling on his part-dry clothes.

While he moved he could sense Josh's gaze was on him, right from leaving the water to the fireside. And he felt sure the old-timer was anxiously wrestling with the emotions of greed against the principles of integrity that must be battling for supremacy within him. Warmth filled Hatton. But, even if they were, he was having few doubts as to how the cookie would finally crumble when Josh made his mind up. Any which way, it would be just a matter of time.

Caleb came up to the fireside and patiently waited for him to finish dressing. Done, Caleb said, 'Hold out your hands. boy.'

The excitement and expectation generated by Josh's steadily disintegrating loyalties died quickly in Hatton. Having to suffer the indignity of rope and manacles again sent anger surging through him.

'Hell, do you have to?' he protested. 'Those irons are cutting my wrists all to hell.'

Caleb's stare was steely and harboured not one ounce of pity. With level voice he said, 'Over the years I warned and pleaded with you constantly not to enter into the life of crime, boy, but you didn't heed me. Now you got to live with the results of it. It's on your own head.'

Hatton glared his contempt, his anger flaring. *The pompous, preaching bastard!* But, what was he doing? His limbs were free. It was one of those chances he'd known would come along. He must hope Josh wouldn't interfere. Impulsively, he swung a fist, a looping right cross which cut in rapidly towards Caleb's exposed jaw. It connected with a soapy thud and sent his ex-partner staggering back to trip over a low rock and hit the ground hard.

Frantically, Hatton dived after him, but Caleb rolled briskly to his right, evading him. He came to his feet dragging out his Colt. His eyes glittered cold fury. Blood was trickling from his mouth and down his chin. He pointed the gun and stared down. He breathed:

'Get on your feet, boy.'

Though seething with frustration at his failure, Hatton rose, grinning nervously. 'Had to give it a try, Caleb,' he said. 'You know that better than anybody.'

Caleb, visibly trembling with anger and glancing at the smear of blood on his left hand, just wiped from his mouth, hissed, 'You did, uh? Why, I ought to . . . ' He paced forward and raised his Colt to strike.

Hatton staggered back, anticipating more pain, but Caleb seemed to take hold of himself, cool his anger. Instead, he relaxed and set about securing

Hatton's wrists and legs.

Hatton grinned. 'Came close to it, huh, Caleb?'

All he got was a glare, and, 'You sicken me, boy.'

Half an hour later, trussed up, Hatton watched Josh build up the fire, then bring a blanket over to drape over him. It smelled of mule. Crane then returned to the other side of the fire and settled himself down. Caleb, on the other hand, had his long back propped against a tree bole. He placed his rifle across his knees while he filled his pipe from his fancy silver tobacco case. His briar packed, Caleb leisurely lighted it, sighed and puffed contentedly.

Hatton faded into a deep, exhausted, sleep.

5

Hatton stared at the pure blue sky. Going on the position of the sun, he reckoned they had been steadily climbing into the mountains for two hours. Already, the fiery orb above was driving up the temperature fast.

Observing Crane, who was leading them, from behind, Hatton came to the conclusion that the sourdough, his pack-mule following him, towed by the lead rope on it, knew the trail they followed like the back of his hand: a narrow, natural groove in the hillside, winding steadily upwards throughout the long ravine they travelled. The path they followed was obviously flattened and widened by the passage of game, migrating over many centuries, after glaciers had gouged it out in times long past.

To his left Hatton observed the drop

was a two-hundred-foot steep slope of conifers, boulders and dead, whitening tree-boles, ending at the edge of a narrow, raging torrent before abruptly rising again, up the other side. A huge cleft had been riven into the mountain range. Hatton now stared up beyond the tree-line, to the barren snowfields on the tops of the peaks. After the desert heat, Hatton found these pleasant mountain temperatures were welcome. But there was no telling, even at these heights, how much the heat would rise to torment him when the sun climbed higher.

He rode relatively easy, for, when they broke camp in the chill mists of the early dawn, for some unsaid reason, Caleb didn't strap him over the saddle as he did yesterday, didn't even tie his feet. What he did do was manacle his hands behind him. Bad enough, but a damn sight better than before. However, the Indian pinto he was on, being frisky, had already pitched him off the blanket-saddle twice and the heavy falls he suffered refreshed his temper, as well as adding to his bruises.

The last time he fell, he damn near rolled down into the ravine. The narrow miss, and his loud, vivid objections to it, broke the serenity of the mountains. He glared up from where he was lying on the edge of the trail and complained bitterly, 'Goddamn it, Caleb, fasten my hands front, will you? Leastways, then, I can hold on to the mane.'

His former partner gazed at him for moments before he dismounted and walked to him, hauled him up and shoved him back on to the primitive Indian saddle.

'You stay as you are, boy,' he said. He walked back to his big black and remounted.

After another half-hour of silent, brooding riding Hatton half-turned in the saddle. He said, 'I need to piss, Caleb.'

Caleb ignored him.

'You hear me, Caleb?' he bawled.

More silence.

After ten minutes of frustration,

Hatton turned again and yelled, 'God-damn it, Caleb, I'm near to wetting myself here.'

Ahead, Josh eased the roan mare he was riding to a stop and turned. The mule halted, too, and dropped its ears and waited patiently. Crane said, 'Gosh-damn, Caleb, all he wants to do is to make water.'

Caleb set his chin, glared. 'I figure it's all about trying something, Josh, and I'm not buying it.'

Josh waved an arm, looked amazed. 'What can he do? Me in front of him, you behind? You think he's going to try and fly outa here?'

The sarcasm apparently lost on him, Caleb said, tersely, 'Along the way he'll have been figuring out some move he can try.'

While enjoying this small spat and hoping to build on it and nourish it, nevertheless Hatton affected a miserable gaze as he looked at the prospector.

'Hell, Josh. No use talking to him. He ain't got an ounce of give nowhere.'

113

Caleb glared, rasped, 'Shut it, boy.'

'But, damn it, I really am pissing myself here, Caleb!' He needed to get Josh's sympathy. and hoped he was succeeding.

Caleb scowled ferociously. 'Then do it,' he growled, 'you'll soon dry out in this heat.' He waved a hand. 'Move on, Josh. Let's get ourselves off this damned ledge. We're too vulnerable here. I've had a prickly feeling down my back for some time. It isn't going away.'

Hatton glared indignantly. 'You and your damned feelings. But it don't matter a damn about me, do it? You know how I feel about fouling myself. Goddamn it, Caleb, like Josh said, I'm manacled, the trail's blocked either side of me and there's a two-hundred-foot drop under my right boot! What in the hell d'you figure I'm going to do? Why, you'll even have to pull out my pecker and put it back when I'm done!'

Josh Crane hooted his derision. 'Yeah. How about that, Caleb?'

But while listening to Josh put in his

two-cents' worth and appreciating his good-humoured jeer, Hatton was astonished to see rock-dust suddenly explode violently off the cliff face, an inch above Caleb's hatted head. Almost immediately afterwards, he heard the boom of a rifle, coming from across the pine-clothed ravine, racketing alien, raucous echoes into the mountains and sending birds crazily flying hither and thither, shrieking warnings. Instantly, Hatton saw his ex-partner's head duck down into his shoulders.

'Damn well knew it!' Caleb roared. 'Move it, Josh! Get on around that bend ahead, pronto. You hear me?'

Howling 'Jesus Holy Christ,' Crane promptly dug heels into the roan's sides and yelled at it to move while he hauled on the pack-mule's rope, causing the beast to trot forward.

Amid the confusion, Hatton's mind worked coolly. Whoever was doing the shooting across there, they clearly wanted Caleb dead and not him. To prevent his one-time partner from moving forward, and to allow the rifleman to get another crack at him, Hatton held the Indian pinto across the trail as best he could, while pretending to try to get it moving. He watched more lead powder the rock face around Caleb; heard more gun noise whack echoes across the brooding peaks of the sierras. But, seeing the rifleman's failure to hit Caleb caused anger to boil up in Hatton. Goddamn it. Couldn't the dumb bastard shoot straight?

Meantime, amongst all the mayhem, Caleb pulled his Winchester from its scabbard and spurred his big black forward. Hatton yelled as his ex-partner drove the horse at his little Indian pinto. As he did so, Caleb was shouting:

'I'm warning you, boy, get that horse moving or I'll shoot it out from under you and you can walk the rest of the way.'

There was little doubt in Hatton's mind that Caleb meant every word. But, always willing to gamble, he howled, 'Jesus, Caleb. I'm doing the best I can.'

Frome hissed, tensely, 'Move it!' He pulled the Winchester .45–90 into his shoulder and fired.

Hatton felt his hat being torn from his head. He watched it float down into the abyss. He knew he wouldn't get another warning. He let the mustang go and it trotted after Crane's roan and pack-mule, already in cover around the bend.

All of them safe behind the towering buttress of rock that formed the angle to the bend, the firing abruptly stopped, making the silence more ominous than the noise. Purposefully, Caleb dismounted. His stare was steel-hard as he directed it at Josh Crane. He pointed a slightly shaking finger at Hatton. 'If he tries anything, shoot him,' he growled.

As was natural to him in adversity — and as he'd discovered at First Manassas when he'd been a boy of fourteen — Hatton grinned his anxiety. In ungainly fashion, he got off his pinto's back and pressed against the ravine wall, content now to await the outcome, but nevertheless still feeling the need to throw a further taunt at his former partner. 'You don't really mean that, do you, old buddy? Shoot me down like a dog?'

Caleb ignored him.

Still smiling Hatton watched Caleb trot back to the angle of rock, edge round it and open up with that fine new Winchester he had. He found he couldn't resist just one more jibe. 'You know you're wasting lead, don't you, old buddy? Goddamn, the times you used to pick me up on that. Umpteen, I'd say.'

Caleb swung around, clearly stung, and aimed his rifle. 'How would it be if I wasted one on you right now, boy?'

Hatton shrugged, offered his slow grin once more. 'No need to get all upset, pardner. Just pointing out what you taught me, that's all.'

Caleb glared. 'That so?' His look turned sardonic. 'Well, don't you go worrying over me, boy, for they've got a rope waiting for you in Santa Fe and five thousand dollars waiting for me. Think on that while you contemplate your wasted life.'

Stung, Hatton turned to Josh Crane. Mingling what he had to say with Caleb's firing he hissed, 'You want to get after that gold, Josh? If you do, go push that no good sonofabitch over the edge right now, or, better still, shoot him while he ain't looking!'

Crane stared. He said, 'You serious?'

'That mine mean nothing to you?' Hatton rasped.

'Sure. But we agreed there'd be no killing.'

Hatton glared. 'Agreed, hell,' he snorted, then stopped himself. No way was Crane going to concur with that notion. 'Yeah, well — you're right, old-timer. He just got me riled up for a second there.'

Cursing under his breath, Hatton turned from Crane and looked once more at his former mentor, while he allowed his quick temper to cool. A moment ago he'd been angry enough to kill Caleb.

He watched Caleb hunch down behind a trailside boulder. His former partner was getting no reply to the lead he was throwing. Hatton felt bitterly disappointed that the bushwhacker had missed, but, his quick temper now under control, the old need to taunt popped up once more. He said, 'Appears to me you've scared him off, Caleb. But, question now is: for how long? I figure he's going to wait a while then pick you off like a dog picks a flea off his back.'

Caleb ignored him and patiently scrutinized the opposite side of the chasm. But sensing the tension in his former partner Hatton grinned and niggled on:

'You sure that posse got all the gang, Caleb? Getting to look as though they missed another one besides me, maybe more.'

Hatton wasn't surprised when he still didn't get a reply. He went on, 'Of course, it could be some other sonofa-bitch bounty man over there — figuring he should be the one to take me in. Five thousand dollars sure is a heap of *dinero*, I guess.' He grinned. 'Damn it, I'm finding it kind of flattering I'm so popular.'

Caleb continued to disregard him.

The ravine became spine-tingling in its quietness. The brooding stillness remained for some time until the birds set to a faltering cheeping again, before slowly breaking into flight amongst the trees and full-blooded nesting-song.

But Caleb still waited. Crouched on this damned ledge Hatton began to realize that, because there was little wind, the sun was now blistering down, despite the altitude. And he had no hat. Finally, his patience gave out.

'Goddamn it, Caleb, can we move from here? He's gone. It's giving me the goose-bumps having to keep gazing at that white water down there.'

'Reckon Hatton's right,' piped up Josh, spitting chaw juice. 'Not only that, another two miles and we'll be into better country all round.'

'You hear him?' Hatton snorted.

Caleb turned, looked at them. To Hatton his old partner seemed more at ease than he had been ten minutes ago. 'I saw him go over the ridge just now,' he said. 'So I reckon it'll be safe enough to move.'

They formed up again and clattered along the ledge, which, Hatton found, was now getting wider by the minute. And, true to what Josh had said, in another half-hour the ravine became shallower and widened out. They descended into a broad valley with plenty of open parkland and sheltering stands of trees. After two hours of steady climbing up the vale they stopped at the edge of a swift-flowing stream.

'Wonder who was doing the shooting?' Hatton said, breaking the silence. He let his pinto drop its head to drink, while feeling it was his duty to try and keep Caleb edgy.

'Curious, uh?' Caleb said, unmoved. He climbed down, let the black loose to drink while he filled all the canteens.

Hatton grinned from the back of the pinto. 'If it'll get me out of this, sure. Hell, wouldn't you be in my position?'

Caleb's gaze was level. 'I ain't in your position, boy, and never likely to be.'

Meantime, Josh groaned as he climbed awkwardly out of the saddle. He growled, 'Damned rheumatics. Ain't the stamina for long rides any more, boys. Like to take my time, these days, let the animals set the pace.'

He allowed the mule and roan to drink, sloshed water over his grizzled beard and face, then drank himself. He smacked his lips appreciatively. 'Sweet, real sweet. Just can't beat mountain water, gents, I got to say.'

Hatton slid off the pinto, dropped to his knees and began drinking, arms still manacled behind him. The pinto nosed the water beside him and slurped. His thirst sated, Hatton grinned at Caleb. 'Seems this Injun hoss might be getting to like me. Guess I do have a way with animals.'

Caleb ignored him and looked at Josh. He said, 'Let's get to moving again, old-timer.'

Seemingly amazed, Josh Crane stared back and complained, 'Right now? Damn it, we only just got here.'

Caleb said, 'Just climb up and lead out, Josh.'

With Caleb's aid, Hatton mounted with difficulty and gazed around him. North, about six miles ahead, in the direction in which they were travelling, the valley floor rose by a thousand feet or more. Beyond that the summit was a bare rocky plateau. It wasn't an easy trail to travel and long drifts of snow remained in the higher hollows. Meantime, muttering, Josh eased into the saddle, collected his mule and headed towards the tableland.

As they rode along Hatton continued to stare up at the forbidding crest. For sure, those boulder-strewn heights were perfect for ambush and once more he began to tingle with expectation. His estimation was they would hit the gap about an hour before dusk.

Now threading through a grove of ponderosa, which crowded against a bluff that stood independently of this narrowing valley, Frome pulled his horse to a stop close to a small, crystal-clear stream that slid down the valley side and chuckled past them. He dismounted and announced:

'We'll camp here, old-timer.'

Crane chuntered, 'Reckon it's past time.'

Deep disappointment filled Hatton. He was expecting to keep going, to have fireworks happen up there in that high country and himself getting free of the irons and clean away. Caleb always did have a habit of fouling things up, knowingly or unknowingly.

'Ain't in such a hurry after all, uh, Caleb?' he said. 'Got something up your sleeve?'

'Climb down, boy,' said Caleb, calmly.

Hatton dismounted awkwardly, his anger simmering. 'Can't you take these cuffs off me for a while?' he said. 'They're cutting my wrists to boot-laces.'

Caleb pushed him roughly to the ground. In moments he had his legs bound together at the ankles. Though he didn't feel remotely like doing so, Hatton forced himself to grin.

'Like I said, old buddy, it's getting to be there ain't an ounce of give in you no how.'

'That's the way it is these days, boy,' said Caleb. As if dismissing him he turned to Josh. 'See to the animals and get supper going, old-timer. I'll be an hour or two.'

'Hour or two?' protested Josh. 'Gosh-darn it, I get to do all the work again?'

'You picked it,' Caleb said. He mounted the big black and rode out.

Hatton met Josh's scowl when the old-timer turned to him. 'Just where in the hell does he think he's going?' the oldster said.

Hatton shrugged. 'Seeing what's ahead, I guess.'

He blinked. *But it really don't matter a damn, do it, Josh? While he's gone, you and me have got some serious talking to do.*

6

Earlier, down the valley, Josh killed two rabbits and was now stirring the stew they made in the pot over the cooking fire. Hatton watched as the prospector produced all the comforts of home from the back of his pack-mule. Josh also dropped into the stewpot salt, beans, wild onions and herbs. The combination of meat and vegetables was already beginning to smell good. Sourdough was baking on a flat stone on the edge of the fire.

'About that map, Josh, and sharing the gold,' Hatton said, lounging uncomfortably against the bole of a spruce Josh had hoisted him against earlier. 'I figure now is as good a time as any — '

Crane scowled, looking frustrated, and cut in, 'I've just been waiting for you to start on that again — and I know I said I'd think on helping you — but I can't get the cuffs off you, can I? I ain't got the key. So there ain't no point in going on about it.'

Hatton allowed his jaw to drop, for effect. 'Never thought of you as a man to make excuses, Josh. Damn it, you could shoot them off. Easy.'

Josh snorted, 'And risk hitting you? They are behind your back, or ain't you noticed? Ten to one I'd blow your ass off trying it. You want that?'

Glowering, the old-timer stirred the big black pot. It seemed to Hatton that the real reason Josh was hedging around the topic was that he was still uneasy about dirtying up his honour by breaking his word to Caleb. Or, he was just plain scared of the bounty hunter. Caleb did have a reputation, no denying.

Hatton shrugged patiently. 'OK, old-timer. But you can at least take these ropes off my ankles for a while.' He looked a little sulky. 'And, damn it, I thought we'd more or less settled a few things last night.'

129

Josh scowled. 'We settled nothing. And it ain't practical right now. Caleb'd go crazy if I freed your feet. You know what he's like. We'll just have to bide our time. Our chance'll come.' He added, 'Last thing we want to do is antagonize him, have him suspect something's going on. Am I right?'

However, Hatton urged, 'Yeah, but, with my feet free, we could still be gone. First place we hit, we could get shut of these manacles. Easy.'

Josh looked belligerent. 'Easy, huh? Everything's so damned easy with you. Caleb'd be on our back trail in no time. I want you with your hands free. I ain't facing Caleb with you handcuffed and out of it.'

Desperation filled Hatton. 'We could do it, I tell you. Give it a chance.'

Josh's stare turned a little more sympathetic, but he said adamantly, 'You ain't thinking straight, boy. Just be patient. There'll come a time and nobody'll get hurt. We've a long way to go. And there's that galoot that's been doing the shooting. Maybe he'll solve your problem for you.'

Hatton scowled. 'And maybe he won't,' he said. 'I know Caleb. He ain't no ordinary man. Anyway, who's to say Caleb will keep his side of the deal with you when you hit Santa Fe? You thought about that possibility, old-timer?'

Crane stared for a moment before he began to pace to and fro, clearly thrown by that prospect. Eventually he shook his head vigorously. 'Naw. Not Caleb. Caleb Frome is straight as an arrow. He wouldn't let me down.'

'Are you saying I will?' Hatton made himself look hurt. 'Well, let me tell you something, Josh. I know different about old Caleb.' He nodded sombrely. 'We go way back. One time, he was just as big an owl hoot as I am right now — but mean, not like me. After the war, in Missouri and Arkansas, he raised pure hell. Want to know something else about him? I was an innocent, callow youth, straight off the farm when we first met. He led me down this path to lawlessness. As God's my judge, Josh, I ain't a natural-born badman. I got suckered into it by Caleb Frome, now I've got to live with the consequences for what bit of life is left to me.'

Crane made a disbelieving noise, shaped his face to match it.

'You expect me to believe that? Why, I've known Caleb as a trail-town lawman, then as a successful rancher until some sonsofbitches razed his place to the ground, burning up his family along with it.' The old sourdough bored his gaze into Hatton's. 'What a god-awful thing for a man to come home to.' Josh stuck out his chin. 'Damn it, boy, I ate at his table more than a time or two, when I was in the hills in that area — was made real welcome.' Josh wagged a confident finger. 'If I know one thing and nothing else about Caleb Frome: when *he* agrees to something, he means it for sure.'

Hatton made his look sincere again.

'Well, I'd like to go along with you, Josh — believe me I would — but, hell, like I say, I know better.' Quizzically, he stared at the old prospector. 'How d'you think he got all that money to buy that ranch and stock it? Do you think he did it by being honest?'

Crane stared resentfully. 'He reckoned so. Said he'd scrimped and saved for ten years to put the money together.'

Hatton chuckled softly, wagged his head. 'Reckon not, old-timer. Crooked dealing, that's how he got it; hiding behind his lawman's badge while he planned jobs. Being the local star-packer, any gold or payroll shipment being made, he'd know about it. He ran a real smooth operation.' Hatton leaned forward, lowered his voice, as if he was about to impart some great secret. 'I tell you, old-timer, in my profession you get to know about things like that — about how the other fellow's doing. The word circulates.' He grinned, shook his head and raised his brows to express his admiration. 'Man, I got to hand it to old Caleb. He sure was a smooth operator.'

Josh stared defiantly. 'I ain't believing you,' he said. 'It ain't true.'

Hatton arched his brows again. 'Suit yourself, Josh. Maybe you've seen the other side of him. Only I know different. See how he slaps me around? He's vicious, clever and a killer. Why, when we were together in the war, he killed for the love of it. It was like a drug to him. And, from the stories I hear, he ain't altered much.'

Josh gazed hard and long. His frown conveyed his doubt. 'You were in the war? Why, you ain't old enough to have been in that shindig.'

Hatton raised brows once more. 'You reckon? Fourteen was old enough to a boy who wanted food in his belly and clothes on his back. All I needed to do was put down a cross on a piece of paper and I was in.'

Josh's eyes widened with an interest that had not been there before.

'The hell you was. You ain't pulling my leg?' he said. 'Soldiering at fourteen? Seems you didn't get to have much of a childhood, account of that.' But his attitude quickly altered again. 'But I've known Caleb a number of years; I've only known you a day or two.' He added confidently, 'I reckon I know who I can believe.'

Hatton sighed heavily. 'Well, can't say I didn't try.' He pursed his lips. 'Pity. Guess that gold'll just have to lie where it is. Millions of dollars, just waiting for somebody to dig it up. And if somebody does get a hand on that map and proves it out . . . ' He shook his head sorrowfully. 'Goddamn it, Josh,' he moaned, 'I just can't bear to think about it.'

Crane scowled and busied himself around the campfire, as if he wanted to be done with the talk.

A few minutes on Hatton said, 'You're offended, ain't you? Because I'm telling you truths you don't want to hear. Well, Josh, you got to believe, I

135

ain't a bad man. I tried — by God how I tried — to go straight after I split with Caleb; just never got the breaks.'

Josh stopped his fussing with camp articles and glared.

'Will you stop it?' he snorted. 'You're making me feel like the back end of a mule. Damn it, you shouldn't go around robbing trains and banks and killing people, then you wouldn't find yourself in the hole you're in.'

Hatton rounded his eyes. 'Killing people? Not me, Josh. But robbing, well I got to hold my hands up to that' — he grinned and shook the shackles behind him — 'if I could, that is. But, I swear to God, I ain't never killed anybody who wasn't out to kill me. And they always got drilled front. Unlike Caleb, who does have a reputation for bringing them in stone-cold dead. Even when I do have to draw my gun, I always aimed to wound. Just ain't in my nature to take life like it don't matter a damn.'

'That's not what they said happened at Saledos Junction,' accused Josh.

'They said you killed an old man sitting in the sun doing nothing more than taking his siesta.'

Hatton growled, 'A damned pack of lies. That was a railroad detective, hoisting up a Colt .45 about to blast me to hell. That's who *he* was!'

'Not how I heard it,' Josh countered.

'Then you heard it wrong, old-timer.'

Crane shuffled on worn boots. 'Yeah, well, maybe . . . ' But, Hatton saw, Josh was clearly worried. The old-timer thought a moment, then shook his head. 'Been doing a deal of thinking, son, since last night. Reckon I've got to stick with Caleb, for my own peace of mind if nothing else.'

Anger fired up through Hatton. He rasped, 'Well, you've sure as hell changed your mind, Jo . . . '

Faint, but crisp, sounds of gunfire, up near the head of the valley, suddenly ripped apart the afternoon calm. It immediately claimed Hatton's complete attention and painted alert lines of expectancy across his sweaty, narrow face. He reared up from the ponderosa bole he was placed against, head cocked and listening keenly.

Josh was saying, alarm on his features, 'Just what in the hell was that?'

Hatton smiled his excitement. 'Maybe my ticket to freedom, old-timer,' he said.

Josh narrowed his gaze, looked a little apprehensive. 'One of your gang?'

'Never did know how many got free of that posse's ambush.' Hatton's eyes gleamed. 'Old Caleb could be wrong about it being none. Those boys of mine are a real tough bunch.'

Josh shuffled nervously. 'If they do win out against Caleb, where will that leave me?'

Hatton grinned disarmingly at the old sourdough. 'Why, free to go, Josh. Damn it, I'll even throw in the map. I ain't got nothing against you.'

Josh looked none too sure about that. 'Nothing?'

'Nothing.'

'But I chucked in with Caleb . . . '

Hatton shrugged as best he could in

his rope and iron restrictions. 'I ain't about to blame a man for that. You saw a sure chance to fund your next trip and took it. What the hell? I ain't a vindictive man. Up to now, you've always treated me fair and square on the trail, backed me on occasion, by God.'

Josh sighed with clear relief. 'Well, guess that's good to know.' He narrowed his eyelids. 'But maybe you're jumping the gun a little. Maybe that shooting could be nothing to do with Caleb getting killed up there. Could be the other way around.'

Hatton pursed his lips. 'A possibility, I guess. Even so, old-timer, like I told you: you're clear. But, if you do change your mind and decide to help me, it won't matter a damn whether he's won or not up there. Either way, you win if you chuck in with me.'

Josh shook his head, began to pace worriedly.

'I ain't never been in a position like this before. Just don't know which way to turn. I got to think hard on it.'

Hatton grinned, relaxed back against the bole of the ponderosa, as best he could. 'Sure, Josh,' he said easily. 'Take as long as you want. But not *too* long. Right? Guess it'll depend on how things have panned out up there. Huh?' His grin was that of a timber wolf.

*　*　*

An hour later Caleb came riding in, leading an Appaloosa stallion with a body draped over the fancy, silver-concho-studded Mexican saddle on its back. First glance, Hatton knew it was one of his gang — Rudi Tavalera, *bandido*, dead as he was ever likely to be.

His hopes sank like a rock in a deep pool. However, there was one heartening feature he could put into the scene: he observed Caleb was dismounting gingerly and with difficulty, like he was carrying lead. When he turned Hatton saw blood was staining the lower part of his ex-partner's shirt and the top of the trousers it was tucked into. Caleb's face was tight-drawn and grey with pain. The wound, it seemed to Hatton, was just above the left hip, through the fleshy part of the waist. The sight warmed Hatton and brought a grin to his face.

'Well, seems old Rudi needed to be close up to get his shot in, if it was him who was doing the shooting in the ravine this morning.' He pursed his lips. 'Too bad he didn't aim a little higher. But, did you really need to kill him, old buddy? You've sure run true to form.' He added, for Josh's ears, 'Yeah, as they say, Bring 'Em in Dead Frome's done it again.'

Caleb scowled at him, but didn't comment.

Josh said, 'You bad hurt, Caleb?'

Caleb gazed at the old-timer. 'Just a nick, old man. It'll heal soon enough.'

Josh looked doubtful. 'Looks more than that to me,' he said.

Caleb began stripping the saddle off

his big black's back. He said, 'Well, it ain't. Take my word on it.'

The sourdough shrugged. 'If you say so.' He nodded to the corpse over the Appaloosa. 'Who's that you got there?'

'Rudi Tavalera.'

Josh raised his brows, waved a hand. 'He ride with Hatton here?'

'He does . . . or did.'

Though Hatton grinned, his anger seethed deep within him because Tavalera had wasted his chance — two chances. But he said, 'Looks like you're losing your touch, Caleb, letting old Rudi put a slug into you.'

Caleb's glance was brief and faintly contemptuous. 'You reckon? Well, you keep your smart talk to yourself, boy, I ain't in the humour for it.'

This time, Hatton grinned across at the old sourdough. 'See what I mean, Josh? Old Caleb does have a tendency to shoot people dead, rather than capture them.' He held his smile. 'Ain't that right, old buddy?'

Caleb's grim face, made ashen with

pain, set into even harder lines.

'I warned you, boy,' he hissed. 'I ain't in the mood.'

Hatton broadened his grin. He said, 'So, what you going to do with old Rudi? Take him into Santa Fe, along with me?'

'Bury him.' This time Caleb's thin lips twitched into a humourless half-smile. 'And, know what, *old buddy*? You get the job.'

Hatton replaced his grin with a vicious scowl. 'Goddamn you, Caleb. You just don't let up, do you?'

Caleb's stare was icy. 'No, boy, I don't. A little like you, I guess, with your snide remarks.'

Annoyed again Hatton watched Caleb turn from him and sit down on the tree-bole Josh had earlier dragged near to the fire, in preparation to toast his rheumatism when the cold of the mountain night closed in.

'Stew smells fine, old-timer,' he commented.

Josh beamed his appreciation. 'The

rabbits I killed this morning.'

Caleb nodded. He said, wincing slightly, 'Beginning to figure it's good you came along. Now, like you to fix my side, if you would. I got bandages and stuff in my saddle bags.'

Hatton scowled. *That's old Caleb. A real prepared man.*

Josh was saying enthusiastically, 'Happy to, Caleb.' And added, 'Looks like you could've lost a deal of blood.'

'Nothing serious.' Caleb peeled off his clothes, exposing his big, finely muscled torso. 'The bullet went straight through the fleshy part, near the hip. Not much more than a scrape. Just needs padding and wrapping.'

Hatton saw, using his war experience of wounds, that there *was* only minor damage done to Caleb. Be sore for a week or two, but would be well on its way to being healed within a month, providing no infection set in.

Armed with bandages and wadding from Caleb's saddle-bags, Josh washed the wound then bound it up, following

Caleb's instructions. The job finished, Caleb slid into a clean shirt and trousers and pulled on his black leather vest.

Ten minutes later, Josh got the coffee going while Caleb undid Hatton's hands and feet, threw him Josh's shovel and ordered him to start using it. Hatton was about to object, but decided he didn't want Caleb's rifle-butt in his ribs again.

To his relief, he found the mountain pasture soil was soft and easy to dig, and, two feet down, to his further comfort, Hatton struck rock. 'Far as I can go,' he said, wiping sweat off his brow and gazing up at Caleb sitting on the tree bole, smoking his pipe, his rifle across his knees, watching him.

'Deep enough for a coyote like him.' Caleb motioned with the rifle. 'Roll him in and tamp him down, boy.'

Hatton scowled but did as he was bidden. When he'd finished, Caleb roped his legs together once more, but left his hands. He gave him a cold smile. 'Don't get excited, boy. It's only while you eat.'

Hatton glared, moodily. 'Like I said, you just ain't got no give any more, Caleb.'

Caleb raised dark brows, as if totally unimpressed. 'See it how you will, son. Won't make no difference to me.'

It was full dark when Josh passed Hatton the rabbit stew. Hatton found he was ravenous and ate like he was. When his plate was clean, Caleb shackled his hands once more. While he did, all Hatton could do was glower right into Caleb's cold grey eyes.

'By God, you once said you wanted me as your son,' he said, bitterly.

Caleb continued to manacle him. 'I meant it, boy. Every word. We could have made a good life together, but you chose not to grasp the opportunity.'

Hatton glared. 'You could've tried harder to convince me, wet-eared kid that I was,' he complained. 'Maybe I would have listened.'

Caleb shook his head, the hard

planes of his pain-paled features full of hollows in the firelight.

'No, you wouldn't, boy. Your mind was made up to ride with Jed Kelly and that was it. Any amount of pleading from me would not have changed that.'

With a grunt he got up and moved away. Trussed up once more, Hatton watched him go to help Josh wash the cooking and eating utensils and stow them; then, as best he could, Caleb carefully cleaned off the blood that had seeped from his wound on to his saddle during his ride back to camp with the corpse of Rudi Tavalera. When he appeared satisfied with his work, Caleb went to curry his black, tethered with the other horses across the clearing. He threw it some of the grass Josh had cut earlier, then commenced the ritual task of grooming his precious, finely muscled Black Velvet.

Knowing he could do nothing but wait his chance, Hatton leaned back and closed his eyes, his growing despair beginning to resemble a cold vacuum deep inside him. It seemed he was never going to be free of Caleb or the prospect of the hangman's noose that awaited him in Santa Fe. At the thought of it, his misery changed to anger. So damn Josh Crane! That sonofabitch sourdough didn't have the guts to take his chances, go for gold!

Hatton tried to calm himself down. He even managed an inward chuckle. Not that there was any gold. There never was a map, there never was a dying old-timer, not that the old coot would ever get to know that. But, it was still a long way to Santa Fe. Maybe he could still get Crane to forget his loyalty and sense of honour and go for the glittering prize he tantalized him with, false though that prize was.

The boom of a rifle close up, shattering the tranquil night, brought Hatton rearing up from the tree bole. He could see Caleb staggering back from currying Black Velvet and falling, hitting his head on the small boulder behind him as he went down. Sprawled in the grass, Caleb lay very still.

For a moment, disbelief ran through Hatton. *Caleb Frome dead?*

On the other side of the fire, chewing Brown Mule, Josh, his eyes round with alarm, yelped. He jumped to his feet and pawed for his rifle leaned against a tree close by.

'Holy cow,' he yelped. 'What . . . ?'

The unfinished sentence was hardly out of his mouth when there was another shot and Hatton watched the top of the sourdough's head blow apart like an overripe melon, the impact sending the old coot sprawling into the hot cooking-fire to lie there smouldering, dead as this morning's rabbit. More confusion, as well as fear, jolted through Hatton. Was he to be next, trussed up like a damned chicken?

His fear subsided rapidly as Shiloh Williams, another member of his gang, moved out of the trees into the firelight. His fat, unshaven cheeks bunched and spread into a grin that stretched from ear to ear.

'Well, howdy, Drew!' he called. 'A fine, fine evening, wouldn't you say?'

Unable to contain his delight, Hatton whooped. 'By God, I just knowed that posse didn't get us all.' He waved his trussed hands, as best he could. 'Get these goddamned irons and rope off me, will you, old buddy?'

With prompt efficiency, Shiloh drew his Bowie and soon had the ankles free. He helped him to his feet. He said, 'Where's the keys to the shackles? You know?'

Hatton nodded. 'In Frome's right vest-pocket.' He stared at Caleb's still body. 'You sure you got him? He ain't playing possum?'

Shiloh's fat face showed smug certainty. 'I got him, Drew. That sonofabitch's killed his last owl hoot. Lay money on it.'

Hatton thought he should feel regret, but oddly he didn't. Caleb's killing was not down to him and he felt that that strangely cleared him of any guilt he might feel. At last, it looked as though the pernicious connection — he often thought of it as an umbilical cord — that held him to Caleb was finally severed. And Shiloh, the Devil bless him, had done the deed.

Feeling as though a great weight was lifted off his shoulders Hatton said, 'So, what happened with Rudi?'

'Crazy greaser.' Williams wiped the back of a grimy hand over his bristled, sweaty face. 'Heard the shooting in the ravine this morning. That's what brung me this way, otherwise I was giving up, figuring we were all dead, apart from me. Connected with Rudi just after noon, though I'd had him in my view ever since he came over the ridge, out of the ravine.' Shiloh waved a hand. 'We watched you work your way up the valley, watched Frome light out after us . . . ' Shiloh paused, scowled, took off his greasy, battered hat and rubbed his shining bald pate with a filthy red handkerchief. 'Shit, Drew,' he went on, 'I told the bean-eating bastard to wait until we got Frome in a cast-iron position so's we could take him out clean, no sweat on our part. But, would he listen? Said Frome killed a *compadre* of his down in Sonora two years ago and he wanted sweet revenge and nothing was going to stop him. Caleb Frome was *his*. You know how that crazy Mexican could be.' Shiloh shrugged. 'Well, I wasn't inclined to play the big hero and Rudi, being useless with a long gun, as we all well know, missed his shot . . . again. Well, by God, it was all true what they said about that sonofabitch' — he nodded towards Caleb's prone figure — 'you don't get a second chance at *him*.'

Hatton stared at the mound of earth he had tamped down earlier over the Mexican. 'Crazy greaser,' he growled. 'Always was the damned showoff.' He turned his gaze back to Williams. 'So, what then, Shiloh?'

Williams lifted sandy brows. 'Well, I laid low, hoping Frome would think there was only one looking for him and he could relax.' He paused and grinned. 'And, by God, he did!'

Hatton nodded approvingly. 'You out-thought him, pardner, sure enough. Now, how about those keys?'

Williams moved across to Caleb's still body and got the key to the manacles, removing the bounty hunter's Colt and stuffing it into his belt just as a precaution; though, Shiloh saw, Frome was dead enough. A great patch of blood covered his chest and when Shiloh moved him, the bounty hunter flopped over as lifeless as a dead fish. He moved back to Drew and unlocked the cuffs.

Hatton rubbed his wrists, waiting for the pins and needles to ease, while basking in the feeling of being able to move without restriction once more, despite the price Caleb had paid for his release.

'Let's get to it,' he said to Shiloh.

After collecting food and taking what cooking and eating utensils they needed

— from the pile stacked tidily by Frome and Crane after washing them — and loading them on to Josh Crane's roan mare, Hatton shot the sourdough's mule. Then, feeling mighty pleased with the night's work, he grinned at his *compañero* and led out.

Armed with his Colt, derringer and rifle once more — Caleb's Colt and fine Winchester .45-90 stashed among the possibles on Josh's mare — Hatton rode Caleb's big horse, Black Velvet. And pleasing him more, Crane's roan, Rudi's Appaloosa and the Indian pinto they herded ahead of them would fetch a good price when they got down to selling them. For he knew a man, John Framer, not fifty miles from here, who wasn't too particular about where good saddlers originally came from. And he and Williams could share the responsibility of keeping the string together, no sweat. The proceeds of the sale ought to tide them over until they could feel it was safe to live off the stolen payroll they'd cached after the Saledos Junction job. And, while waiting for that event, he could organize another gang. There were plenty of good men out there whom he could approach and sign up.

Of course, Shiloh would still have the pocket money they shared before stashing the loot, as did he — now he had Caleb's saddle-bags at the back of him, the place where Caleb had put most of the stuff he had taken from him upon capture.

Hatton grinned his pleasure. Things were definitely looking up.

7

Pain jarring his head where he fell against the rock, blood feeling wet and sticky where it trickled down the back of his neck, Caleb played possum and listened, hardly breathing, while horses travelled past him. When he thought it was safe he risked a quick glance, even though his vision was blurred and he was feeling weak and groggy. Vaguely, he made out the backs of Drew and another man, riding out, while herding what other horses there were left before them — out into the dark night shrouding this high valley. It was when their noise finally faded that Caleb became aware of the fierce pain in his chest.

He wondered why he was still alive. He remembered the impact of the bullet hitting him, flinging him back into the rock he found himself sprawled out against. But now the danger appeared to be over, it didn't take him long to figure out that hitting the small boulder had knocked him out. It had probably saved his life, too — lulling Drew, and the man riding with him, into a false sense of security. Most likely they assumed he was dead.

So, why wasn't he dead? He fumbled at the point of the pain in his chest and pulled out his silver tobacco-case from his shirt-pocket. The bullet that should have ripped his heart apart had bent and mangled the case, before ricocheting off across his ribs, scraping them enough to cause sufficient blood to flow to make it look as though the bullet had hit the right place and penetrated deep. He swallowed on his very dry throat. It was very clear that the solid construction of the tobacco-case had saved his life and he would never be so lucky again.

As the waves of nausea still troubling him cleared, he fumbled for his handgun. Not there, of course. And, for a moment, a flame of fierce anger welled up in him. Like a wet-eared tenderfoot, he had allowed this to happen, ignoring the first rule in his mental book on personal safety: *you never take anything for granted; you follow everything through*. Even though Tavalera was dead, he should have kept looking. In dropping his guard and assuming much, he had left himself open to a sucker punch and got it. Just now, providence, not hard-won skills, saved him from certain death.

With the sounds of the horses now gone and his vision clearing, he cautiously rose, his trouble-senses keyed up to their highest pitch. He looked around. Nothing to suggest danger, but it wasn't long before he became aware of the sickly-sweet smell of burning flesh. He glanced quickly in the direction the camp-fire. What he saw flipped his gut — Josh Crane, burning.

With a disgusted growl, he staggered over and dragged the sourdough's smouldering body out of the flames, while ignoring the hot agony his movements showered through his head and body.

He stared down at Josh's exposed, charred flesh, where it was beginning to cook. It was no way to go, even though the bloody ruin of the old-timer's skull told him the sourdough hadn't suffered the agonies of burning. That meant a hell of a lot to him, for he knew of others who had burnt. *Others who were precious to him.*

But he was in trouble, no doubt about that. Further perusal of the campsite told him the mule was dead — a useful animal to have anywhere and a damn-fool thing to do, killing it — looking at it from his own point of view, that was. The horses and saddles were gone, too. Top of that, he knew, without looking, that he was left unarmed and without food. Stood to reason Drew and his companion would take what victuals there were, and for sure, they'd never leave good weapons behind, even though it seemed they'd presumed he was dead. And the missing horses meant he would be afoot for some considerable time. What the distance was to the nearest habitation he could only guess at. However, a brief, but thorough scan around the camp-ground established that Drew and his buddy had, in some ways, been neglectful. An enterprising man could make much of what was left lying around.

He stared at the dome of night sky above, the stars shining in the crystal-clear mountain air. Another plus, he noticed, was the unrisen moon beginning to pale the eastern horizon. Soon, it would be poking its face above the line of white peaks, whose bright tips he could see up above the dark, vanilla-scented ponderosas that surrounded most of this valley until you got to the high ridges. A clear, moonlit sky would be a mighty useful start to the manhunt he was about to embark upon.

His muzziness fully cleared, he

stripped off his shirt, bathed the bullet-crease across his ribs in the stream — dabbing it clean with his handkerchief, while wincing at the pain he was already suffering from the wound Tavalera had put into him this afternoon, in the fleshy part of his waist.

To his relief he saw that the gash made by the ricochet off his tobacco-case — though stingingly painful — was superficial and, all being well, would soon heal. But, causing him more hurt than the other two wounds put together, the large, ugly red patch where the bullet had impacted on the tobacco-case, almost directly over his heart, was now throbbing viciously. It was already beginning to discolour.

He tried to close his mind against his miseries. He must get moving. There was much to do and skulking here was not going to get it done. The head wound caused by hitting the boulder he would leave to its own devices. He could feel the blood was already crusting over it, indicating bleeding was almost at an end and — hopefully — wouldn't become a real concern.

A search soon found abandoned bandages, obviously dragged out of his saddle-bags by Drew to make room for things he considered of more use. As best he could he dressed the long ragged scrape across his ribs. Then after more hunting around, he found Josh's shovel, no doubt discarded — also as useless — by Drew and his owl-hoot friend. Though it would mean using time he didn't have, Caleb felt compelled to give Josh Crane a decent burial and he did so. Half an hour later, and dripping with sweat, he threw the shovel aside, after tamping down the earth over the old-timer's body.

Next, he found a knife — the slim, sharp blade Josh had used to skin animals, as well as cut up vegetables and such like when in camp. A further search discovered a length of thin, plaited rawhide, plus a bag of coffee beans. Moments later he came upon a large water canteen. Better still, he located a cooking-pot, a coffee-pot and a sack to carry them in. In fact, all the comforts of home.

Figured I'd taught you better, Drew, he thought. And the only answer to such oversights, as he could think of, was that his one-time protégé must definitely have assumed that his old partner was dead. He always did have more confidence than was good for him, did Drew; tended to be sadly inattentive to what Caleb Frome always considered to be important detail. *Real bad characteristic, boy.* However, he tried not to think of his own shortcomings of this afternoon — not checking the possibility that the Mexican could have a companion nearby. But, unlike Drew, he would learn from it. He would never, ever make the same mistake again.

He tucked the knife into his belt and wrapped the rawhide rope across his broad shoulders. He filled the canteen at the brook, tinkling soothingly past what had been a reasonably contented camp a while ago, with everybody getting ready to settle down for the night. In a strange way, he found the tranquillity it inspired odd. Another thing: already, it was as though nothing had happened here. It was as if Nature dismissed the puny, insignificant follies of Man and continued to slumber in her mountain vastness — while accepting the wounds made in her soil to receive the bodies of Tavalera and Josh Crane. Caleb narrowed his eyelids. *Those born of the earth shall return to it*, so the Bible said, if he remembered the phrasing correctly. It didn't really matter a damn if he didn't. It fitted for him.

He didn't give the campsite, or even Josh's grave, a backward look as he paced off into the night, taking the direction Drew and his companion had adopted. The dead were dead. For those really dear to him he reserved a special place within him; a part of him that would never forget, that would be with him always. The deep, early grief a man felt, he had long-since established, was best left by the grave when the ceremonies were over. The need for revenge would go on.

The moon was now risen, helping him to follow the trail left by Drew and his sidekick.

There were all sorts of clues to pick up regarding the owl hoots' passage through the trees — disturbed pine-needles, scraped-off bark leaving a light-brown scar, cracked branches. Crossing the moonlit meadows, there were grasses and blossoms flattened, making clear tracks for him to follow. And, by the clues he found, it was clear that Drew and his companion were not expecting to be followed. Caleb allowed himself a smile. It would be useful for them to keep thinking that way.

Two days on, he paused on the last craggy slopes of the manzanita-and-paloverde-sprinkled foothills tailing out from the mountains. Footsore and aching but fed on rabbit snared with the rawhide rope that Drew and his sidekick had left behind and having plenty of water to drink, Caleb felt in reasonable shape.

Pausing on the flat top of a gaunt bluff he looked into the hazy distance. Drew and his *compañero* had been kind, leaving him a trail a blind man could follow and dawdling along — having themselves long camp stops — as though tomorrow would do. Because of that he was as certain as a man could be that he wasn't far behind them. They must be feeling very sure he was dead.

On the dry plain he looked for signs of dwellings but saw nothing, just shimmering heat over a sepia expanse, reaching away to seeming infinity from these ragged foothills. He knew there was habitation down there — squat, neat adobes mostly, lived in by Mexican farmers and their families, with their goats and sheep. They were well able to extract a living from that inhospitable land. For, though it looked a dry waste, he knew there were springs and patches of verdure that would sustain modest herds, or flocks. These, he knew from long acquaintance, the Mexican farmers exploited to the full.

He scrambled down the last of the rocks and on to the desert floor. Ignoring the pains in his blistered feet and wounded body, he strove to lengthen his stride. An hour later, he couldn't believe his luck. He broke out of the cacti and thorny brush into a cleared area around a low, flat-roofed adobe. It was clearly Mexican in style, with a clay cooking oven outside, standing apart from the dwelling. The oven was open on all sides, but covered by a brush canopy. A water well was close by. The damp area around it said water was recently drawn from it.

'*Hola*, the house,' he called. He took off his widebrimmed, brown hat and mopped his peeling brow.

After a minute staring expectantly at the dark maw of the open doorway to the house, suspicion and slight alarm began rising in him. It was unusual not to have some greeting, usually welcoming, when visiting these lonely *casas*. However, his gut tightened as a heavily accented demand suddenly came floating out from a large clump of prickly pear, some fifty yards to his left. 'Lift your hands high, *señor*,' the voice sing-songed. 'If you do not, I will kill you.'

Caleb stiffened. Raising his arms and holding them away from his body he said, 'I am unarmed, *mi amigo*. I have not come here to harm you.'

A grunt came from the patch of pear. 'I can see no guns, that is true. But that does not say you have none.'

'I would not deceive you.'

A harsh, cynical laugh floated from the prickly pear. 'I have only your word for that.'

Caleb very quickly suspected trouble recently visited this place. Drew and his sidekick?

'Agreed,' he said. He made a gesture with his upraised arms. 'I regret not using the customary courtesies of your people, but I am urgently seeking two men, driving horses. They are bad men and I need to know if they came this way. The tracks I have followed say yes.'

There was a silence, then, 'They came this way.'

'How long ago?'

'Two hours. Perhaps a little more.'

A trickle of excitement seeped through Caleb. He said, 'That is good news. Now, if I may presume further: I need water, food. I am willing to pay. I also need a horse.'

'They needed food and water, too.' Sounds of discomfort came from the patch of prickly pear, a gasping grunt of pain.

Caleb said, 'You sound distressed. Tell me what has happened here. I would like to know, but I find it difficult — talking to the cactus.'

More time elapsed — maybe half a minute — before a small Mexican rose from the prickly pear. The man was clothed in dirty white cotton — a smock and baggy trousers, with a narrow leather belt around his middle. He carried a mean-looking machete in his right hand. But, shocked, Caleb observed that the man's face was a swollen mess. Ugly bruises deformed his brown features. His right eye was puffed and shut tight — a lump the size of a bantam's egg swelled the right side of his jaw. Dried blood caked on numerous cuts.

'They have taken my daughter, Josefina,' the farmer said.

Setting his jaw into a grim line, Caleb said, 'The men I asked about?'

'Two men driving three horses,' the Mexican said. 'A roan, an Appaloosa, a small Indian pinto. One man rode a big, fine black horse.'

Black Velvet?

'What did they do to your daughter?' he said.

The farmer shrugged. 'Who knows? They came smiling. One man, he smile nearly all the time.' Caleb felt his gut tighten up. *Drew?* The Mexican was saying, 'As is our custom we gave them food, water. But while they ate, they kept looking at my daughter. Right away, I saw evil in them. I started to pray they would finish their food then continue their journey. It was not to be. They began fondling my Josefina.' Caleb saw anguish fill the farmer's battered features, a look of helplessness. 'I could do nothing, *señor*,' he went on, 'but attack them with my hands. I did not have my machete. It was in the house and I dared not fetch it. I fought until they beat me unconscious with their guns. After that' . . . An aura of great anger suddenly seemed to begin to emanate from the small Mexican. 'Rest assured, *señor*' — his voice trembled a little as he spoke — 'when I catch them, I will kill them.'

Caleb made a gesture with his hand. 'Are you sure they took her? She hasn't run into the brush to escape them?'

The Mexican shook his head. 'No. I have called for her. She does not come. Believe me, they have taken her.'

Caleb narrowed his gaze. He said, 'If it is so, accept my *simpatia*. Together, we will make them pay.'

'I will make them pay!' The farmer straightened his thin body — his posture hostile. 'Words,' he spat. 'Is that all you *gringos* have? Your *simpatia*! It does not bring my daughter back.'

Caleb tightened his lips before he said, 'No. But at the moment, it's all I have.' Caleb met the Mexican's one-eyed stare with sincerity. And he found he was not offended by the derogatory term, *gringo*. The man had good cause.

The farmer seemed to relent a little, too; calm down. 'I am sorry, *señor*. But I find my trust of the *Americano* is not good at the moment.'

Caleb said, 'Understandable.' *He had to get moving*. He continued to stare straight at the Mexican. The man was clearly still angry and obviously deeply concerned about his daughter, Josefina. Maybe he could harness that. 'I assume you are familiar with the desert, *señor*?' he said.

The Mexican frowned, looked puzzled. 'Of course.'

Caleb nodded. 'Well, I suspect the men who have taken your daughter are the ones I seek. With your help, I intend to catch them. And, may God allow, when we do find them, your daughter will be found unhurt.'

The farmer crossed himself fervently. 'May God allow.' Then his look changed to one of scorn. 'But, you are unarmed.' He waved an arm. 'They are well armed with *pistolas* and rifles. You talk of catching them, punishing them?' He waved a disparaging arm. 'What with? Pah! The *Americano*! He is a crazy man.'

'Have you guns?' Caleb said.

The Mexican shook his head, waved the machete in his hand. 'I have only this. Hardly enough. But I will follow them to the ends of the earth.'

Caleb rubbed his chin. He stared at the small farmer. 'Is there a town nearby? A place where we could buy horses, weapons?'

'Not close, but we can get horses.' The farmer waved a hand towards the north. 'The *Americano*, John Framer. He live that way. He has a ranch by Welcome Springs. He catch horses. He trade horses. *Any* horses.' The farmer made his look significant. '*Comprendes, señor?*'

Caleb stared hard. 'Stolen horses?'

The Mexican nodded. 'So it is said.'

Caleb stared. 'Interesting. Will you take me there? I've got a feeling the two men we seek may have headed that way.'

The farmer's unbruised eye took on a new, hard aspect. He weighted the machete in his brown fist. Caleb decided the gesture possessed great eloquence.

'If that is true, *señor*,' the farmer said, 'and we are fortunate, they will pay with their blood, whether my daughter is alive or dead. There was a time I fought with Benito Juárez.' He stuck out his chest. 'So, you see, I am no stranger to fighting, though it is some time ago now since those glorious days.'

Small and insignificant though he was, the man impressed Caleb. 'Well, you have cause enough to feel that way, my friend,' he said. 'But the young one; the one who smiles: I want to take him alive. The Santa Fe Railroad and the Territory authorities need him badly. He has several crimes to answer for. Rest assured, a noose awaits him.' He raised dark, sweat-soaked brows. 'As for the other one. If your daughter is — we must pray that it is not so — but if the worst is discovered, feel free to handle him as you wish. Do we have a deal?'

The farmer seemed torn for moments, but it also appeared he was a man who could weigh up a situation and come to a quick decision. He nodded firmly.

'It is a deal.'

'Good.' Caleb offered his hand. 'Now, I am Caleb Frome.'

The farmer paused for a second or two before taking the offered paw. It was clear it was an unusual event in his life to have an American offer such a gesture of friendship. 'Esteban Campos,' he said. He spoke the name proudly before a frown clouded his fatty brow. 'You are Caleb Frome, the bounty hunter?'

'Yes.'

'Your name is known in this country. Some say you are a devil.'

Caleb's look was impassive. 'Only by those who have done wrong and have to pay for their crimes,' he said.

The farmer smiled, despite his bruises. 'Perhaps that is so.'

Caleb briskly straightened himself to his full six feet three. 'Now, food, Esteban. I am in need of a good meal.'

'My daughter had prepared *estofado* (stew). It was to be our supper. You are at liberty to share what is left. Though I think the gringos ate most of it.'

'It will be more than welcome.'

It was found there was some left, enough for the two of them. Ensconced at the rough-hewn table in the *casa*, Caleb ate his meal hungrily. Esteban ate hurriedly before he busied himself putting food into a sack. Then he went out and filled a water-skin and the canteen at the well. But his sudden call startled Caleb.

'Maria!'

Made abruptly interested, Caleb hurried to the door. A woman? That could complicate matters. A complication he didn't want. Standing on the bare ground outside he stared at the farmer.

'I thought you were alone.'

Esteban turned his battered face to him. 'I am. My wife, she is dead some years — from the fever. My two sons, they are gone to Mexico City. I do not see them any more.' He attempted a bruised grin which deformed his features and revealed large brown teeth. 'My sons. Maybe they are *bandidos*. Who knows? As for Maria' — he grinned more — 'she is my *burro*. She is out there somewhere. When she is not needed, I turn her loose to find food. She come, soon.'

Caleb gasped, 'A donkey?'

'*Sì*.' Esteban held his grin. 'I was going to call her, to go after those *puercos* (pigs).' He made a fierce gesture at the desert. 'But I heard you approaching through the brush and . . . well, you know the rest, señor.'

Caleb smiled grimly. 'You are a man of surprises, Esteban.'

The farmer grinned. 'It has been said.'

Caleb nodded. 'So, I think it's about time we paid Señor John Framer a visit. You reckon?'

'With the *burro*, two hours and we will be there.' Esteban gestured. 'But, you have wounds. Maybe I could dress them?'

Caleb's answer was abrupt. 'They'll do for now. The welfare of your daughter is of more importance.'

Esteban's stare was searching this time, respectful. 'You are an unusual man, Señor Frome.'

It was Caleb's turn to grin this time. 'It has been said, *señor*.'

'*Si*.'

Though clearly sharing his humour, Esteban went into the house without another word. Seconds later he came out with his machete sheathed in leather. He stuck it in his belt.

'Maria,' he shouted again. This time a bray came from the brush. Moments later the donkey appeared.

The Mexican grinned again. 'You see, Caleb Frome? Maria!'

Caleb again smiled. 'I see for sure, Esteban Campos.'

8

Esteban insisted Caleb climb up on to the burro. With seemingly inexhaustible stamina, the Mexican loped along beside the trotting beast, while explaining: when he was young he was taken by the Mescalero Apache and was raised by them. They taught him a way of life that had served him well throughout his days.

Dusk was settling over the drylands when they topped the rise overlooking Welcome Springs. Down the slope, about a quarter of a mile away, stood Framer's small, adobe-built ranch, amid clusters of dusty greenery. Cottonwoods grouped around the large pool that, Caleb assumed, must be Welcome Springs. Eroded irrigation channels probed out across the desert from the lagoon — probably dug by Spanish friars in past times — to take water to crops, but were now just feeding pastures of grass and thriving sagebrush — when anybody bothered to let water into them, that was. Which didn't appear to be often. If there was an adobe mission here once, it was now returned to dust and become part of this country's wild and bloody past. And, judging from Esteban's account of Framer, he was a shady dealer, trading mostly in horses, moving them quickly, while not looking too closely at their history.

Without the need for words, he and Esteban bellied down just below the crest of the hill. Yellow light shone from the two unglazed front windows of the small ranch house. It said the shutters were not yet closed, to allow what evening air there was to continue wafting into the house. Horses were in the corral near the house. They were eating hay that was thrown down for them. One was drinking at a trough, set into the corral. Caleb could see a big black horse was amongst them. It had to be Black Velvet.

By his side Esteban said, 'In the corral, those are the horses the men we seek rode and drove.'

Caleb nodded. 'Figured that.'

Estaban went on, a sneer in his voice, 'Framer, he thinks himself a clever man. He keeps some horses hidden, in a canyon fed by springs — over there.' The Mexican pointed a brown finger at the ramparts of red rock rising out of the desert about five miles away.

Again, Caleb nodded. 'Figures.'

Under the makeshift gallery running the length of the ranch house, he could see three men sitting on a bench, leaning their backs against the adobe wall. They appeared to be smoking tobacco and taking in the last colours of the day, purples, reds, yellows, daubed by the fiery ball that was the sun, hanging close to the western horizon. It was obvious the men were drinking hard liquor, too, judging by the bottle being passed between them.

Better and better, thought Caleb.

'I do not see Josefina,' said Esteban.

'She was not left on the trail,' said Caleb, 'so there is still hope.'

'True,' admitted Esteban. As Caleb looked at the Mexican sideways he saw the farmer's battered features betrayed nothing of what he was thinking, or feeling.

They waited, watching the country grow deep mauve and take on an air of mystery as the sun crept nearer to the horizon. Ten minutes later, Caleb watched one of the men get up and walk to the corral. He appeared to be smoking a stogie. Reaching the peeled rails the hombre leaned against them and seemed to be continuing to drink in the beauty of the evening. The other two, who were on the bench, went into the ranch house. Their faint laughter carried to himself and Esteban on the near-still air. Without much effort Caleb identified Drew as being one of them.

Going to be an interesting night.

Esteban said, 'I go down to the

corral. The man leaning there: I will kill him.'

'Is it Framer?' quizzed Caleb

Esteban shook his head. 'One of the gringos who took Josefina. A bald, dirty man with fat cheeks. I think he does not shave very often. The smiling one we agreed would be yours went into the house with Framer.'

Caleb raised a brow, scrubbed his own neglected beard, as he looked at the Mexican. 'You going to Indian up on your man?'

Esteban fingered the haft of his machete. 'That is my intention.'

Caleb nodded. 'Guess I'll try and move in on the ranch house. Come in the back way, if there is one.'

'There is,' Esteban said.

Caleb nodded his satisfaction. 'Just one thing I ask, *mi amigo*: don't make your move until you observe I'm close to the house. I think there will be enough light left for you to be able to see me.'

'I will *hear* you, *señor*, if I do not see

184

you,' said Esteban.

Caleb narrowed his eyelids as he looked at the Mexican. Well, he did say he was trained by the Apache. He nodded. 'I believe you. If you can kill the man quiet, do it, then let out a whoop to distract those in the house. That will give me chance to move in on them and complete the surprise.'

A smile creased Esteban's battered face. There was a lust for revenge in the grin.

'When you move in, you will distract them also,' he said. 'They will not know which way to look for the danger. And maybe I will have a gun when I have killed the gringo dog' — he gestured fiercely — 'and, who knows what good fortune that will bring to us, uh?'

Caleb frowned rubbed his bristled chin once more. He said, 'Got a feeling it isn't going to be that easy, *compadre*. And remember, the smiling one is mine.'

Esteban's look was sober, even a little offended that Caleb should bring his integrity into question at this time. 'It was agreed, *señor*. You do not accept the word of a *greaser*?' Esteban used his own mocking emphasis on the derogatory term used by Americans to denote Mexicans.

Feeling slightly chastened, Caleb said, 'Of course. It is just that I am eager to have him face American law in an American court.'

'That, too, was understood,' Esteban said. 'Now, something else . . . I have a feeling my Josefina is in the house, and that she is safe.'

Caleb nodded, though he didn't have much faith in such purported mystical powers. 'Let us hope it is so,' he said.

Of a sudden, Caleb felt the pressure of Esteban's hand on his arm. When he looked at the Mexican he saw that the stare, from his bruise-free eye, was intense, accentuated by the multiplicity of colours given off by the near-set sun.

'It is time to go,' he said. 'I wish you good hunting Caleb Frome.'

Caleb said, soberly, 'And you, Esteban.' He felt the need to add, '*Vaja con Dios.*'

Esteban's gaze was searching, as if looking to see if the good wishes were sincere. He seemed to think they were. He nodded his bruised head. 'And you, *mi amigo.*'

Like a shadow, Esteban slid into the growing dusk. It was as though the desert just swallowed him up. The sun set, deepening the shadows. A whippoorwill called sleepily from the cottonwoods by the gently bubbling spring. It caused Caleb a moment's disquiet. When it called again, he relaxed. He had little doubt it was a goatsucker and not Indian. There hadn't been any Indian trouble for some years in this section of the country and he felt Esteban would have known of their presence in any case and would have let him know.

Caleb gazed down at the ranch house and hardened his resolution. Setting his chin into a stern line he took a deep breath and moved along just below the brow of the rise. He thought: *I'm coming, Drew boy; better believe it.*

As he had already planned in his mind, he would take a long, wide arc and sneak up on the rear of the adobe ranch house, through the mesquite. He saw no reason why the plan should fail. And with the revelation that Esteban had been brought up by the Apache, he entertained few doubts that the Mexican would also accomplish his intended manoeuvre — taking out the man enjoying his stogie by the corral with consummate efficiency, unless the outlaw was possessed with a hyper-awareness. Not impossible, having lived an owl hoot life where sharp senses and quick reactions often meant the difference between life or death — *as now*.

Frogs were starting to make noise down around the water-hole. He didn't ponder how they got there. They made an eerie, harsh cackle. There was the possibility, if he made his way through those trees to the back of the house, that they would stop their racket, which could be a warning to the house — and the man at the corral, sucking on his cigar — that things were not all they seemed on this tranquil night.

With infinite patience he threaded his way through the brush. The frogs didn't stop their racket.

By the time he was within a hundred yards of the ranch house, it was near dark. Issuing from the dwelling came ribald, drunken laughter, a lot of coarse talk. Caleb found little trouble in picking out Drew's hearty guffaw. But the sudden terrified scream of a female in trouble from within changed everything rapidly.

He heard Esteban's anguished Indian whoop go up. It sounded as though the Mexican wasn't able to contain himself once that anguished cry rent the night. Caleb heard a scuffle by the corral, the roar of gunfire, the harsh gasp of a man hurt, then a kind of peculiar silence that was pregnant with menace.

Forgetting all caution, and his blistered, painful feet, Caleb ran as best he could towards the ranch house. At the one unglazed window he looked in. A pretty dark-haired girl was sprawled on a rough cot and cowering against the dirty wall behind her, her black eyes wide with terror. Almost in the same instant he saw Drew's crouched back disappearing as he went out through the front door. Drew was clearly wanting to know what was happening outside, or was he going to make a run for it? The man whom Caleb must assume was Framer was standing in the centre of the big room, Colt lined on the girl while staring with alarmed eyes after Drew as he went through the doorway. Caleb could see Framer's erect manhood, standing out from his open flies.

It said it all.

Without thinking he dived through the glassless window. He came up fighting. Framer was turning, his brutal face startled. Caleb hit him on the side of his neck with a large fist. Framer yelled harshly. His Colt went off, but the shot went wide. Caleb hit him again, brutally, compressing all his revulsion, frustration and revenge for his recent suffering into the blow. Though Framer was not one of the men who had caused it, he was thinking of other things equally repulsive to a decent man which had been about to be performed on the girl had he not intervened just now.

With a harsh cry, Framer went down to the dirt floor. His Colt fell out of his hand and hit the ground with a dull thud. Caleb kicked him this time, a vicious driving swing that hit Framer full on the jaw. With a moan the crooked horse trader flopped to the earth floor's hard pan, unconscious and out of it. With fierce intent, Caleb picked up Framer's Colt.

In two bounds he was at the door. In the yellow light shafting out of the two front windows Caleb saw a bald-headed man slumped against the corral rails, his eyes staring wide open, his hand-held Colt limp on his lap. Blood was streaming from a terrible gash in his neck and shoulder. Sadly, Esteban was sprawled lifeless nearby, blood covering his chest, machete still in his hand.

Drew was standing on the cleared ground before the ranch house, peering towards the corral, his lean back framed in the yellow lamplight. He was calling, obviously unaware of anything amiss behind him.

'Shiloh? The hell's going on?'

'Turn around, boy,' Caleb ordered, harshly.

With a strangled cry, and with cougar-sharp reactions, Drew dropped to the ground and rolled to his left. 'Git him, Shiloh!' he bawled as he went down.

Williams, Caleb saw, was lifting a Colt, lining it up. Despite his awful wound, the damned fool was grinning.

'I'll get him, Drew,' he was calling. 'Betcha.'

Caleb fired Framer's Colt. The shot ploughed dirt a foot to the right of the grinning owl hoot. Cold clamped Caleb's flat stomach. *Goddamn, that's what you get having to use an unfamiliar gun!*

The thoughts ringing in his head, Caleb cocked the unfamiliar Colt once more, adjusted his aim. While he did, Shiloh was firing, but Caleb saw his hand was wobbling. He heard the back-trail rider's shot hammer into the adobe wall behind him. As if now played out, Shiloh slumped, his arms spread, his chin resting on his chest, his mouth agape. Blood dripped from it.

Caleb swung around. Drew was running to a big sorrel already standing saddled at the tie rail over by the small barn. An old owl-hoot trick — always keeping a saddled horse or two close to hand, ready for instant flight.

'I said hold it, boy,' he roared, 'or I shoot!'

'You can't do it, Caleb,' Drew shouted, dust swirling about him. He laughed. 'You know it, I do.' He vaulted into the saddle.

'Don't bank on it,' warned Caleb. 'I can maim you, boy.'

By this time Drew was spurring away. 'See you in hell, Caleb!' he yelled as the night swallowed him up.

Enraged, Caleb swung on the man sprawled against the corral fence. He paced forward and kicked the gun out of his hand, knocked off his hat. He grasped the flap of hair that the *hombre* had obviously pulled over his bald patch to vainly try and hide it. He drew the owl hoot up, close to his blazing eyes. The smell of booze and unwashed flesh that issued from him was rank.

'What's your name, mister?' he rasped.

The outlaw bored his stare across the narrow space between them. An odd contempt veined the steel-hard glare. 'Go to hell, Frome,' he said harshly.

Caleb banged his head against a corral post, hard enough to cause the owl hoot to yell:

'Shiloh Williams, for Chris'sake. Damn you, can't you even let a man die in peace?'

Caleb relaxed his grip, but not before slamming Shiloh's head back against the corral post once more.

'Thought so, when Drew hollered out your first name. Can't say your poster likeness flatters you, Williams.'

Shiloh stared. It was as though some hidden energy suddenly revitalized him, caused him to come alive again. Hatred reeded his stare. He bared bloody, brown, broken teeth.

'You think I give a damn?' he rasped. He pawed at the awful wound in his throat and shoulder. 'Look what that damned greaser's just gone and done to me, the no-good sonofabitch.'

Caleb found he didn't have an ounce of sympathy for the dirty, murderous-looking outlaw. 'You should have left his daughter alone,' he barked.

Shiloh made an attempt at a guffaw. 'You reckon? Well, I ain't had me a female in near three months. She had it coming, flouncing herself around that god-damned hovel they called a home. Goddamn, these greaser bastards make you sick. They's just begging for it, seems to me, and she got it.'

Of a sudden, the owl hoot went limp. To Caleb, besides being fairly drunk, Shiloh looked to be driven to the edge of death through loss of blood. A large pool of it was already spreading under him and gradually sinking down into the hard pan. Shiloh's eyes dropped shut. But after moments, he came alive again.

'Got some news for you, Frome,' he mumbled. He gave off a laugh that gurgled on the blood in his throat.

'And that is?' Caleb demanded harshly.

'You had a ranch in Colorado — the C bar F. Right?'

Caleb felt icy fingers clamp his gut. He leaned forward. 'You know something about that?' he hissed.

'Old Drew,' went on Shiloh. 'You know'd him real well once. True?'

'Where's this going, Williams?'

Shiloh's tortured stare became intense as it lifted up. 'That ranch of yours,' he said. 'It was us that fired it.' He grinned. 'Old Drew . . . well, he was the sport that put the bullets into your wife and kid. Didn't want to see them suffer. How you feeling now, bounty hunter? Haw, haw — '

Williams's ghastly laughing ended abruptly as Caleb's bullet blew his skull apart. He made sure he didn't have trouble with his aim this time. But, the deed over, Caleb felt a terrible weakness begin to flood through him. Williams's bitter, derisory words set all the ghosts rising again.

Drew killed his wife and child?

Caleb made a strangled noise that struggled to get past his constricted throat. Drew was responsible for the destruction of his life? Was responsible for this hollowed out shell of a man he had become? The hollow shell that once housed a happy, fulfilled man? His cry of anguish ravaged the desert night. But it was Josefina's harsh scream that dragged him out of his desperate, grinding misery.

'Behind you, *señor*!'

When he swung around, Caleb saw Framer was in the doorway of the adobe, yellow lamplight framing him. Blood was streaming from his nose. His manhood was still hanging out of his trouser front. He seemed oblivious to that fact. He held a rifle in his hand and was bringing it to his shoulder. He was mouthing curses.

Caleb triggered, saw his shot take the horse trader clean through the brisket. Framer grunted and jack-knifed, blood spurting. The Winchester dropped from his hand as he clutched at his chest. The rifle hit the earth floor of the gallery with a dull thud. The horse trader's limp body followed the weapon down to end up crumpled and motionless on the hardpan.

It was then that Josefina came out of the ranch house, straight into Caleb's arms. He winced as she hit his bruises and wounds, gritted his teeth against the shock. She seemed to take it for granted he'd come here to rescue her.

After seconds he said, easing her away from him, 'Are you Josefina?'

She met his steady gaze. He saw her dark, beautiful eyes were filled with tears, mostly of joy. '*Sí*,' she said. Then she looked around and added, still with pleasure, 'Where is my father? He must have come with you. He would not leave me to these men.'

He tried to stop her peering around his big body, but couldn't. What she saw caused a stark cry to break from her. She must have seen Esteban's bloody body. She broke away from him and ran to the still form.

'*Padre*!'

Caleb moved to her. When he arrived at her side she was already kneeling by Esteban's body and was hugging him to her breast, her own head pressed against his. She did not seem to mind the blood that was being transferred to her white blouse and red skirt.

'I am sorry it ended like this, *señorita*,' he said. The words seemed so inadequate. 'Your father — he was a brave man.'

Heartrending sobbing answered him. He could only stand helpless. For years now, such misery-causing things had made no sense to him. If there was a God, how could he allow things like this to happen? Wasn't he supposed to have universal compassion, gentleness? Caleb compressed his lips. Maybe somebody could give him the answer. For he, sure as hell, didn't have one. All he knew was the pain.

He waited for what seemed an hour, though it was probably just a few minutes. He would let the girl have her grief. But one solid, burning quest now possessed him after Shiloh Williams's shattering revelations.

He had to find Drew.

9

When Josefina had finally cried herself out, Caleb gently told her the story of how he came to be here with her father. When he'd finished, he said:

'You have other family near, Josefina? Somebody I can take you to?'

Her red-rimmed eyes turned up. The dark orbs were full of pain, but she pulled herself together and lifted her chin proudly. '*Sí*. In Quemada Flats. Three hours ride, that way.' She waved a vague hand towards the now dark west.

Caleb said, 'You will lead me there?'

'*Sí*.'

Caleb said, 'We will take your father there, for burial.'

Josefina's head lowered. She played with her hands. After moments she looked up and said, 'It will be right. My father has brothers, sisters there — my uncles, aunts.' Her eyes became more alert, grateful. 'I thank you, Señor Frome, for making the time to take me there. Surely you want to be after the gringo pig who got away?'

'Yes, I do.' Caleb gently placed his hands on her shoulders. He put her age at about sixteen. 'But there's time for that. Now, rest until I have things ready.' What came to his mind next was more of an afterthought, but, if what he had in mind had been done to her, he was sure it would not be an afterthought to Josefina. For her it was probably devastating. 'Did they . . . abuse you, Josefina?'

The girl coloured under her creamy complexion, bit her lower lip, quickly looked away. After moments she said, 'On the way to Welcome Springs. The one with the bald head. I tried to fight him off, but he was too strong. The laughing one — he just grin, make joke about it. He is a pig!'

Caleb thought: *For sure, you should have beat the hell out of the sonofabitch for doing that to the girl, Drew boy. But I guess you're well past that kind of thing now. Maybe, you were waiting your turn in the ranch house. Just being a bit more patient. Seems nothing I ever taught you stuck.*

Caleb pressured Josefina's shoulders gently, as if in an attempt to try and instil some of his own strength into her.

'The man is dead, *señorita*. Your father killed him. Think on that and put it behind you, if you can.'

Fierce light came to Josefina's dark eyes. 'May he rot in hell, Señor Frome,' she hissed. 'Such a man will not ruin my life! But, my family. That is another matter.' She slumped her slim shoulders and went silent.

Caleb steered her towards the bench, placed hard against the ranch house wall, under the gallery. She sank wearily down on to it. It did not seem to matter to her that her blouse and skirt were red with her father's blood. Rather, she seemed proud of the fact.

'The bald one, Josefina,' Caleb said quietly, 'what he did to you. Be sure, only I will know of this. If your relatives want to know, the outlaws did not touch you. Do you understand me?'

Her sad, dark eyes rolled up to meet his gaze. Her gratitude was clear. Impulsively, she clutched his hand, pressed it against her cheek. He felt her warm kiss on it before she said, '*Gracias*, Señor Frome. *Mucho gracias*.' She shook her head. Her loose raven hair brushed across her shoulders. 'I fear my uncles, though kind, are not so understanding about such things. They still live by the old ways. And, because it was a gringo who has done this, who knows what they will do, say, if they get to know about it?' She shrugged. 'My father, I do not think he would have minded. Maybe the Apache taught him a different way. Who knows?'

'Who knows indeed,' said Caleb. He looked down at her olive-pale, heart-shaped face. For all her outward appearances of using her inner courage to fight her grief and rape, she looked a very lonely, withdrawn figure sitting on the bench. He said, 'Now, I have to prepare for our journey to Quemada Flats, Josefina.'

'I understand, *señor*,' she said. She looked like a lost little girl, sitting there. 'Please do not let me delay you. Believe me, my life will not ruined by this.'

Brave words from a brave girl.

At the corral, Caleb found that Black Velvet was pleased to see him. The gelding nuzzled him, made horsy noises of pleasure. After a brief reunion of patting and fussing, a search of the barn found his saddle. He set it on Black Velvet's broad back. A further reconnoitre of the storehouse revealed that it held most of the stuff Drew and his owl-hoot friend took from the camp in the mountains. He soon uncovered another saddle and placed it on Josh Crane's roan, for Josefina. It looked to be Josh's saddle. A further search and Caleb found his handgun and holster, but he discovered his Winchester .45–90 was missing. It didn't surprise him. Drew always did have an eye for a superior gun. He pursed his lips. He would have to take what he knew was the boy's piece, propped against one of the stalls. It was one of the latest Winchester .44s and well kept. He rammed the long gun into his saddle scabbard. It would do.

Next he lashed Esteban's body to the back of the Mexican's *burro*, Maria. She didn't like it but eventually became resigned to it. Shiloh Williams and John Framer he left where they lay.

He went to Josefina. 'Ready to go, *señorita*.'

She nodded numbly and rose. She seemed calm, composed. But when she saw the blood on his shirt, her beautiful eyes rounded.

'You are hurt, Señor Frome,' she exclaimed. 'Was it from the fight?'

He shook his head. 'No. Another time. It doesn't matter now.'

Her eyes remained dark orbs of

surprise. 'But it does matter! You are bleeding!'

Caleb looked down at his grimy clothing. New blood *was* seeping through his shirt and through the waist of his pants.

'It'll be OK,' he said.

'It is *not* OK, señor,' Josefina protested. It was as though she was looking for some useful thing to do to maybe take her mind off things, or compensate him for all the inconvenience she maybe thought she was putting him to. 'If only to honour my father, I must fix your wounds.'

'I'd rather get on,' he insisted, shuffling his feet impatiently.

She bent, fumbled under her ankle-length red skirt. She pulled down a white underskirt, dexterously preserving her modesty by some adroit manoeuvring. Clear of her body, she held the garment in her hands. 'Come into the house,' she said, 'where there is light and I can see to dress your wounds.'

Caleb sighed. 'There's really no need for this, Josefina.'

'I will not hear such talk!' She gestured impatiently. 'Come, Señor Frome,' she pleaded. 'While we argue, I could be wrapping your wounds.'

Caleb sighed resignedly, gazed at her imploring, but defiant, face. She clearly was not taking no for an answer. And he was mature enough to know it was not wise to argue with a female — even one as young as Josefina appeared to be — once her mind was made up. Maybe she did see it as some kind of payment for taking part in her rescue, tragic though that turned out to be, for her. And the wounds, he must admit, probably *were* in need of second-party attention. It was only a rough job he'd made of dressing them back in the mountains.

He followed her into the ranch house and submitted to her wishes. When he stripped off his shirt, she gasped when she saw the massive purple and yellow bruising, the jagged scar across his chest and the ugly hip wound. 'You say you do not need help, *señor*?' she scorned. '*Dios mio*! I think different.'

She busily set to work.

★   ★   ★

They made good time to Quemada Flats. Even so, it was early morning by the time they reached it. Caleb saw, beneath the bright, cold moon, that the south side of the settlement — where they happened to be — was a huddled collection of square, white, adobe dwellings. To the north were false-fronted buildings and tarpaper shacks, lining what would be called Main Street, though it was nothing more than a trail that ran straight through the centre of town and out into the desert again. It was like a dozen other Anglo-Mexican settlements that he knew of. There were embellishments. Amenities to the south included a plaza for parading and trading, a cantina, a smithy, and a church with the traditional bell tower to call the faithful. To the north were two Anglo-type hotel-saloons. And at the far north end, a livery stable. Slap-bang centre of it all was a general store.

At one of the first adobes, Josefina stopped her roan, dismounted with sinewy ease and tapped on the stout door. It was opened by a small brown man with dark, greying hair and a drooping moustache of like colour. His swarthy face and frown quickly expressed his surprise.

'Josefina!' he said. He stared at Caleb, then at the body over the donkey, Maria. 'Is that Esteban?' He returned his questioning stare to Josefina. 'What has happened to your father, *mi querida*?'

Josefina said, 'In a moment, Uncle.' She turned to Caleb. 'This is one of my uncles, Felipe Campos. Uncle, this is Caleb Frome.'

Caleb nodded at the Mexican. '*Señor*.'

Felipe eyed him cautiously. 'I have heard of you, Señor Frome,' he said curtly. 'You hunt men for the bounty on their heads.'

Caleb nodded again. 'That is so.'

'But not this time!' said Josefina. She quickly went in to explain what had happened at her father's farm and the rescue at Welcome Springs, but not the rape in-between.

When she finished, Felipe said, 'Your are untouched, *querida*?'

'I am intact, Uncle,' said Josefina.

Felipe appeared to find immediate relief in that. Caleb was pleased Josefina could lie so convincingly. He didn't want the sort of complications the discovery of rape could maybe lead to in a closed community like this. Or was he imagining things? Nevertheless, he would see justice was done. Josefina should have no worries on that score.

A glance up told him other people were now crowded in the doorway of the large adobe, behind Felipe. Two boys and a girl, a woman and an old man. They seemed to be listening intently to everything that was said. But, with the preliminaries cleared up, within moments Caleb found himself hustled inside — the horses and the donkey with the body still on it spirited away by one of the boys and the old man. The door closed quickly behind him and Josefina.

Seeing the horses being led away, Caleb said, not attempting to hide his concern, 'I need the black pronto, Señor Campos. I would like it to remain here.'

'Seen outside this door a fine horse like that would attract attention we do not want at the moment, *señor*,' explained Felipe. 'Where it will be corralled is not far. It can be returned quickly. It will be fed and watered. Is that not good?'

Though still a little uneasy, Caleb nodded. 'Yes. It is good. And I thank you, Señor Campos, for your reassurance.'

Felipe bowed his head slightly, as if

accepting his reluctant appreciation.

'*Gracias*. Now,' he added, 'may I offer the hospitality of my house?' Felipe gestured towards the rough table in the centre of the room, around which were five heavy chairs. Caleb seated himself in one.

'Thank you, *señor*,' he said.

Sitting there, Caleb's bristled, fatigued features etched themselves strongly in the light of four candles in wall-holders around the room. Another candle stood on the table. Josefina moved away into the next room, prompted by the women. After moments, not surprisingly, the chatter of females came from what was probably the kitchen. Naturally, they wanted to know *everything* from Josefina. Would they get it?

Caleb soon found himself sipping a potent brew offered to him by Felipe. Moments later the older woman came in with a plate of food. Caleb ate with relish the hotly spiced meat-and-vegetable stew laid before him.

Watching him eat, Felipe said, 'The

gringo who got away. From Josefina's description, I think he is here, *señor*. She would not know him because Esteban did not come into the town very often with Josefina and the gringo was probably not here when he did.'

Immediately, Caleb paused in his eating, his spoon half-way to his lips. 'How can you be certain of this?'

'Two hours ago, a gringo rode in. It is said his horse appeared to have been ridden hard. He headed for the gringo saloon, the Double Eagle. We know him here as the *bandido*, Drew Hatton. Over the years he and his *pistoleros* occasionally stop here on their way to Mexico, presumably after a robbery.'

Caleb's stare hardened. 'Is there no law here to stop them?'

Felipe shrugged. 'A county deputy, he rides in once a week, to see that things are OK.' He waved a vague hand north. 'The gringos up there, they say everything is all right, so it is. Our word does not matter. Because of this Quemada Flats is a haven for the wrongdoer and the *Americanos* make plenty of money keeping their mouths shut and their cantinas open. Do you understand me, Señor Frome?'

Caleb rubbed his darkly bristled chin. 'Indeed I do.' He stood up. 'But, if this is so, I'd be obliged if you would show me this saloon, *señor*. I most certainly have business with that man.'

Felipe's dark stare and swarthy features hardened. 'And so have we, Señor Frome — my nephews and their fathers, my brothers; those of Josefina's blood.' He passed a finger across his throat, his dark face intense. 'Together, we will kill the gringo ourselves. You must appreciate Esteban's blood has to be avenged.' Then he waved a deferential hand. 'Naturally, we will be grateful for ever for your assistance in returning Josefina safely to us and unharmed, but the right of vengeance must be ours.'

Caleb felt his gut tighten, his stubborn streak steel up. *Drew Hatton was his, by God.* But he must remain cool, try and reason with the man.

'I can understand your need for revenge, *señor*,' he said, 'but I have ridden a long way to capture Hatton, not kill him. When Esteban — your brother — and I rode out after them, I got an assurance from him that when we caught up with the kidnappers Hatton would be my prisoner. As far as I am concerned, that still stands.'

Felipe set his dark features into determined lines. 'But Esteban is dead and that changes things.' He tried to make his face look amenable, but his demeanour, Caleb noticed, took on a look quite as obdurate as his own. 'Again, on behalf of my family, I thank you a thousand times, but the revenge still must be ours.'

Caleb stared at the small Mexican. 'Maybe if I explained a few things, *senor*,' he said. He went on to narrate — despite the pain it would cause him — the tragedy brought upon his family by Drew and his vicious gang at the C bar F ranch — revealed to him through Shiloh Williams's sneering lips only hours ago. The tragedy told, he finished: 'So, on the basis of that, *mi amigo*, who do you think has the greater need for vengeance?'

Felipe's dark gaze studied him. Caleb thought he detected a certain sympathy in those deep eyes and swarthy features.

After moments Felipe said, 'In the light of what you say, *señor*, this is not an easy decision any more. However, things must remain as they are. The need of the Campos family to avenge wrongs done to them are deep-rooted in our traditions and cannot be violated.'

'As they are in mine!' protested Caleb. 'You do not have the monopoly. But, be that as it may, I also have to respect the laws of the United States, whose jurisdiction, I must remind you, you are now under. I need to see Drew Hatton hang for *all* his crimes, not just the wrong done to my family, and yours. If it will help your decision, I can assure you, he did not kill your brother. Esteban himself killed the man who killed him. A man called Shiloh Williams.'

'But he kidnapped Josefina. That is enough.'

Nevertheless, Felipe shuffled. He looked undecided. He diverted his gaze and spoke in rapid Spanish to someone whom Caleb had not realized was behind him. He turned quickly. He was surprised to see the old man had returned and was holding a shotgun on him. He must have made his way back after dealing with the horses, crept in through the kitchen. Caleb certainly hadn't heard him return to the room. Indignant, he swivelled his angry stare back to Felipe.

'I am disappointed, *señor*,' he said, 'that you feel the need to talk so rapidly in your own language so that I cannot follow you.'

And, clearly agitated, Josefina came into the room. It was obvious she had been listening in the next room to what Felipe was saying to the old man. 'No, Uncle! Señor Frome is our friend. This cannot be right.'

Though he looked embarrassed, Felipe rapped, '*Silencio*! I will have to talk with your other uncles. I need their opinions.' He went into rapid Spanish again. As he spoke, Josefina's eyes widened.

When he finished she said, 'But there is no decision to make, Uncle. Señor Frome has the right. We cannot deny him the gringo *bandido*.'

The old man's voice, firm and hard, rapped, 'Go into the kitchen, *querida*. This is man's business.'

'I will not!'

'Go!'

Bursting into tears, Josefina ran out.

The old man eyed Caleb. 'For your benefit, *señor*, I will use *Americano*. I have no wish to deceive you.' He turned to Felipe. 'Fetch your brothers, my son. They will need to know what is to be done with the gringo, Hatton. I have decided we will take him from the hotel and into the desert. After that, he will not be heard of or seen again.' He turned his gaze back to Caleb. 'And, rest assured, his dying will not be easy, because I have it in my mind that Josefina is not telling us the whole truth. Be that as it may, to make certain justice is done, the gringo must die and by our hands. Surely, you can understand this?'

Rage came up into the back of Caleb's throat. 'Drew Hatton is mine, old man,' he gritted.

He reached for his Colt, but the old Mexican cocked the lined-up shotgun. 'That would not be a wise thing to do, *señor*,' he said. 'And I have no wish to kill you.' He glanced at his son. 'Take Señor Frome's gun, *hijo*. We will lock him in the storehouse until this is over.'

More rage ran heat through Caleb. 'You will regret this, old man,' he breathed. 'I have tried to be reasonable.'

The old man shrugged. 'Each day brings fresh problems, Señor Frome. Perhaps when you have thought quietly about this matter, it will not be so difficult to accept. I hope so. We all walk towards the same goal. Only the end will be different.'

'You don't understand,' Caleb protested. 'He is . . . '

Josefina rushed into the room once more, holding her hands imploringly out to her grandfather. 'Do not do this, *abuelo*!' she pleaded. She grabbed hold of his right arm.

The agitated older woman came bustling in. 'Josefina! Come away!'

Caleb saw his chance. The old man was distracted. Felipe hadn't taken his gun from its holster yet. He pulled his Colt, intending not to kill the old man but take the initiative. Pain hammered across the back of his head and he cried out harshly.

As a Stygian blackness bubbled up to swallow him into its dark depths, he could hear Josefina screaming.

10

'Señor Frome! Señor Frome!'

Caleb realized it was Josefina's urgent whisper that was making him drag himself out of this claggy mire of semi-consciousness he found himself in.

'Señor Frome! Wake up!'

He tried to brush away what appeared to be cobwebs draping themselves across his eyes. He became aware of pain hammering across his head. His wounds were aching with brutal persistence, too. Reality began the dribble back to him in little, reluctant pieces. He became aware of Josefina untying bonds that were around his hands and ankles. It was dark where he was. There was the smell of leather, spices, cheeses, the whisper of rodents scuttling. The storeroom? The old man said he should be locked in here while they dealt with Drew.

Drew!

He reared up. 'What has happened, Josefina?'

'I will tell you in a minute,' she said as she undid the last of his bonds. She fumbled down by her side. 'I have your gun here, *señor*.'

She lifted up the Colt and held it out. Caleb took it gratefully, checked the loads. It was full.

'Thank you, *señorita*,' he said. 'Now, what's happened?'

She shrugged. The silver moonbeams coming in from the door ajar behind her etched her pleasing shape in their light. 'It is simple. My uncle — Felipe — when you threatened to shoot my grandfather, he hit you with his gun — '

'You know I would not have killed your *abuelo*, Josefina.'

'*Si*,' she said. 'But my uncle didn't.'

Caleb accepted the logic of that. He said, 'All I wanted to do was get away so they would not get Drew Hatton.'

In the darkness, Josefina's voice was puzzled. 'What is so important to you concerning such a bad man? It does not make sense to me.'

Caleb struggled to his feet, swayed as nausea hit him. He found support against the storeroom wall close by. He waited for his head to clear.

Josefina urged, 'Tell me, señor.'

Ignoring her plea Caleb said, 'How long have I been here?'

'Half an hour.'

'Have your family gone to get Drew Hatton?'

'As far as I know, they are still talking as to the best way to capture him. He has friends here and he is in the gringo part of town. It will be difficult.'

Caleb glanced through the half-open door. There was plenty of moonlight out there, but dawn could not be far away.

'Where is my horse, Josefina?'

'I will take you to it only if you will tell me why Drew Hatton is so important to you.' She sounded ada-mant — a bit like a petulant little girl.

Damnation! The need to bargain with such a slip of a girl caused a momentary flare of anger to rise in him, but he soon quelled it. In a peculiar way, he felt she had the right to know.

'I will tell you on the way to the horse,' he bartered.

'*Sí*. OK,' she said. A ghost of a smile flicked across her wide lips. Walking through the moonlight, she paced slightly ahead, leading him. He briefly, quietly, told her the story. When he finished she said in a whisper, a frown creasing her smooth brow, 'You wanted to make him your son, *señor*?'

They were now creeping through the night past square, white adobes, taking the well-used lanes between them. All were silent.

'Yes,' he said. 'But,' he added bitterly, 'instead, he chose the lawless trail.'

Josefina gestured with bare brown arms and said, 'Yet, your feelings are still strong for him.'

'I guess so. Or at least they were until I heard he was involved in the killing of my family.'

'Now you want to kill him,' she said.

'No. I want to see justice done, Josefina,' he said.

'Yes, to hang him — kill him.'

'Not me. The law will decide.'

'Suppose he does not want to hang? Suppose he wants to kill *you*? Wants to fight it out with guns.'

Caleb shrugged. 'It's not what I want.'

'Then your heart is still big for him,' she stated. Her eyes were round as they studied him. 'And this make a coward of you, *sí*?'

Damn the girl!

'He's a killer. One way or another, he'll pay the price.' He added, with a touch of harsh anger, 'Now leave it be.'

They were past the adobe *casas* now, weaving through the sagebrush. Caleb saw a corral looming ahead, horses in them. It told him that maybe the Campos men had not yet made a decision regarding Drew. He could hope. He saw Black Velvet.

'Where will my saddle be, Josefina?' he said.

She waved at an adobe building, attached to the corral. 'In there, I think.'

He strode towards it. Soon he found his saddle. Surprisingly, Drew's Winchester was still in the scabbard. Inspection told him it was still fully loaded, too. He went out to the corral and quietly called Black Velvet. The gelding came eagerly. Caleb saddled him quickly.

'Hatton . . . he did not hurt me,' Josefina said suddenly, breaking the quiet. 'That says he is not all bad.'

She was trying to defend him?

'He didn't stop Williams,' he said gruffly.

She lowered her eyes. 'That is true.'

Caleb scowled. 'And, you ever pause to think he was maybe holding on to join in the fun with Framer, in the ranch house? He was in there. You saw what Framer intended to do to you, before I killed him.'

Josefina's face looked shocked. She lowered her gaze. 'Do you think so? But Hatton, he smiled all the time, like the world was a joke.'

'A rattlesnake has a smile on its face, too,' said Caleb. 'I beg you to remember that, before your girlish sympathies run away with you again where men like Drew Hatton are concerned.'

He swung up on to Black Velvet and looked down at her, his face sombre. '*Vaja con Dios*, Josefina,' he said. 'I hope you don't get into too much trouble with your family.'

She said quickly, 'I will come with you. I can still help. I can distract the night clerk at the Double Eagle, where Hatton is staying. While I do, you can sneak up to the gringo's room and arrest him.'

Simple, huh? thought Caleb.

'This is not a game, girl,' he said. 'There is danger in it.'

'I know,' she said. 'But — '

'No buts. I will handle it.'

She stamped her foot. 'I want to help, Señor Caleb. Please.'

Caleb shook his head. 'You have done enough, girl. Now go back to your family. This is man's work.'

She pouted and blurted, 'But if it is true what you say that he was going to do things to me, I have a right — '

'But he didn't,' interrupted Caleb. 'And that's the difference.'

He tugged Black Velvet around harder than he need have done and headed up towards the main street. He encountered no one as he made his way to the Double Eagle. Inside, there was a light in the foyer. Off to the left — in what looked to be the saloon — a card game was still in progress.

He paused, stared into the room through the open door, hung with open draught curtains. Four men were around the green baize. Drinks were beside hands with fans of cards in them; blue cigar smoke hovered around the shaded lamp above the table. A heavy game of poker was in progress by the look of it. A lot of money was changing hands. And Drew Hatton was sitting in, brash as you like. Caleb stared. *Crazy kid.*

The clerk, who had looked to be fast asleep behind the desk when he walked in, called from behind him, 'Can I help you, mister?'

Caleb stared at him. 'I guess not. I've found what I'm looking for.'

He didn't even look at the clerk. He kept his stare on Drew. Drew was pausing, as though he instinctively knew he was there in the foyer, looking at him. When their gazes clashed, Caleb saw Drew's shoulders tense, his pale gaze harden, panic slightly. Then Drew was throwing cards aside, rearing up and pushing his chair away while streaking a clawed hand for his gun.

Caleb already had his Colt out. 'Hold it right there, Drew. It's over.'

Lead hissed a death song past his right ear, accompanied by the boom of Drew's Colt. Caleb went into a crouch.

'Don't make me kill you, boy!' he shouted.

With the bark of the gun, confusion reigned. The card players were scattering, seeking cover behind any sturdy barricade there was available. Amid the flurry of bodies, Drew was running towards a door off to the right.

'Hold it right there, damn you!' ordered Caleb.

Drew's laugh came as he closed the door behind him. A gun cracked nearby. Lead buzzed near Caleb's left cheek. Caleb swung. The shooter was peering over an upturned table. Caleb hammered lead through its flimsy top. The pistol man grunted and flopped back. A quick glare around told Caleb nobody else seemed inclined to take up where the gunman had left off. He pounded across the saloon to the door through which Drew had gone.

He didn't hesitate. He went through it and booted across what appeared to be an office. There was a desk, a brass-studded, red leather rotating chair behind it. There was a door ahead. He plunged through it.

Drew was in the trash-filled alley, which was overgrown with weeds. He was running up and down, as if bewildered. 'Where's my damned horse?' he was repeating. 'Where's my damned horse?'

Caleb halted his run. 'Don't make a bad move, Drew, or this time I won't aim wide.'

The boy stopped his pathetic running and turned. His grin switched on.

'Caleb! Well, ain't this a surprise.'

Caleb didn't appreciate the joke. 'Why are you here? You could have been gone, boy,' he said. 'You always did live too near the edge.'

'Ain't it a fact.'

Still smiling, Drew pulled out the makings. He rolled a quirly, pulled a match up his pants and fired the tube of tobacco, cool as you like. While he was doing it he was saying, 'I had the sorrel tied up out here. Just don't know where it could have got to. You know anything about it, Caleb?'

Frome shook his head. 'No. Seems to have all backfired on you, uh, boy?'

'Don't usually.' Drew took another draw at his quirly. 'Well, what you going to to, Caleb? You know damn well you ain't taking me back alive.'

'I got to, boy.'

Drew laughed, but it was a nervous laugh. 'You ain't doing it, you hear me? Even if I got to kill you.'

'I'm thinking you won't do that.'

Drew's smile was now gone. Moodily, he puffed at his quirly. 'You damn well think so? How's this?' He cocked and fired the Colt in his hand, snake-fast. Caleb realized he was firing his own piece as Drew's lead ripped through his lower arm. It sent his lead wide, sizzling into the lightening dawn sky. With a gasp he dropped the .45 and grasped his bleeding arm.

The smile returned to Drew's tight features. 'Jesus, you're a hard-dying man, Caleb,' he said. 'You must have nine lives. Back in the mountains, you were left for dead. Goddamn you, why didn't you leave it at that?'

'At the C bar F ranch, you killed my wife, and daughter, boy.' Caleb gritted his teeth. The pain in his arm was already excruciating.

The smile on Hatton's lips disintegrated. 'What sonofabitch told you that?' he rapped harshly.

'Shiloh.'

'Shiloh!' Drew's eyes were round, mad, in the half light of pre-dawn. 'Did he tell you it was an accident, that I did them a favour? Did he tell you that?'

Caleb stared. 'You're awful sick, boy. Maybe I can get you into a home somewhere? Maybe I can have a word with the authorities.'

Drew stared. 'A home? What sort of a damn home?' He waved his Colt, his face a waxen mask. 'See what I mean? It's you. Running my life again. And you saying I'm sick?' He stabbed out with his Colt. 'It's you that's sick. Chasing me all over the goddamned universe, with your morals seeping out of you like a great load of green horseshit. Couldn't you have left it? Gone the other way? No!' He glared, giggled. 'Well, you know what, Caleb? I've made up my mind. I'm going to kill you. Do you a favour. What d'you think of that?'

Drew cocked the Colt. Caleb could only stare at him.

The boom of a gun shattered the peace of Quemada Flats once more. Caleb flinched automatically, but it was Drew who was staggering. Caleb was amazed to see red blood was already beginning to cover the boy's chest. Drew flopped down. He was pawing at the ghastly, open wound as if he didn't believe it.

Still stunned, Caleb stared towards where he saw the gun flash. It was the old man of the Campos clan. He held a smoking shotgun. Beside him was Josefina, holding the bridle on Drew's sorrel. No wonder the boy couldn't find it. *She must have removed it to stop him leaving.*

'He was going to kill you, *señor*,' the old man said.

Caleb knelt down beside Drew and gently prised the gun out of his hand. Drew turned his grey stare up to him.

'Where did it all go wrong, boy?' Caleb said.

Drew said, 'First day we met, Caleb. That's when it all went wrong.' He smiled a bloody smile before his eyes rolled up and he died.

Though he didn't want to admit it, Caleb said, 'I reckon you could be right, boy.'

He went off to find a doctor after he'd arranged to have the boy buried decently.

THE END

A TOWN CALLED TROUBLESOME

John Dyson

Matt Matthews had carved his ranch out of the wild Wyoming frontier. But he had his troubles. The big blow of '86 was catastrophic, with dead beeves littering the plains, and the oncoming winter presaged worse. On top of this, a gang of desperadoes had moved into the Snake River valley, killing, raping and rustling. All Matt can do is to take on the killers single-handed. But will he escape the hail of lead?

CABEL

Paul K. McAfee

Josh Cabel returned home from the Civil War to find his family all murdered by rioting members of Quantrill's band. The hunt for the killers led Josh to Colorado City where, after months of searching, he finally settled down to work on a ranch nearby. He saved the life of an Indian, who led him to a cache of weapons waiting for Sitting Bull's attack on the Whites. His involvement threw Cabel into grave danger. When the final confrontation came, who had the fastest — and deadlier — draw?

RIVERBOAT

Alan C. Porter

When Rufus Blake died he was found to be carrying a gold bar from a Confederate gold shipment that had disappeared twenty years before. This inspires Wes Hardiman and Ben Travis to swap horse and trail for a riverboat, the *River Queen*, on the Mississippi, in an effort to find the missing gold. Cord Duval is set on destroying the *River Queen* and he has the power and the gunmen to do it. Guns blaze as Hardiman and Travis attempt to unravel the mystery and stay alive.

MCKINNEY'S LAW

Mike Stotter

McKinney didn't count on coming across a dead body in the middle of Texas. He was about to become involved in an ever-deepening mystery. The renegade Comanche warrior, Black Eagle, was on the loose, creating havoc; he didn't appear in McKinney's plans at all, not until the Comanche forced himself into his life. The US Army gave McKinney some relief to his problems, but it also added to them, and with two old friends McKinney set about bringing justice through his own law.

BLACK RIVER

Adam Wright

John Dyer has come to the insignificant little town of Black River to destroy the last living reminder of his dark past. He has come to kill. Jack Hart is determined to stop him. Only he knows the terrible truth that has driven Dyer here, and he knows that only he can beat Dyer in a gunfight. Ex-lawman Brad Harris is after Dyer too — to avenge his family. The stage is set for madness, death and vengeance.